MW01518764

SEITKA'S SHIFTER

HEALER SERIES - BOOK FOUR

CHAR CAULEY

BLUSHING BOOKS

Blushing Books® Publications
is an imprint of
ABCD Graphics and Design, Inc.
A Virginia Corporation

977 Seminole Trail #233
Charlottesville, VA 22901
The trademark Blushing Books®
is registered in the US Patent and Trademark Office.

Char Cauley
Seitka's Shifter

EBook ISBN: 978-1-61258-955-8
Print ISBN: 978-1-61258-973-2
Cover Art by ABCD Graphics & Design

CONTENTS

THE HEALER'S SHIFTER

*S*eitka kept running, leaping from tree branch to tree branch as fast as she could. She didn't know who was chasing her, but they were taunting her, telling her they would capture her and what they would do to her. They were telling her she couldn't escape. Her heart was racing, her breath deep and rapid. How could she have been so stupid? Why did she not listen to her brother? All she wanted was some horehound for the children, to ease their cough. She could have used a drop of whiskey and honey, but she liked the horehound better, for children. She had wandered further from her village than she had thought and had become confused as to which path to take to head back home.

Suddenly, she was accosted by a pack of wildcats from the enemy camp. Cearul was their leader, and his name fit him perfectly. He was a fierce fighter. Even her brother, Colin, tried to stay out of his way. While in human form, Cearul was very handsome—big and strong. But after spending any time with him, a person would know something was not right with him. He liked to fight and to hurt others. It gave him pleasure to see others in pain.

When he was in animal form, he was vicious, always rolling the younger kits, snapping at them until they left the food alone and wandered off hungry. He was always this way, Seitka had heard, a bully to the younger and weaker cats. That is how he ruled, by fear.

Seitka immediately took to the trees as she was faster as an animal. She was smaller and sleeker. They chased her further from safety and closer to their camp. She knew her situation was hopeless. She had just come into heat for the first time yesterday. Her brother had warned her to stay in their home as any male could smell her, and she was so pretty, it was almost impossible for any male cat to resist her.

Suddenly, she was knocked to the ground from behind. She rolled, her belly in the air and her throat an easy target, but that is not what any of the males were thinking of.

Five huge, black, wild male cats circled her, each wanting a turn to mate her, whether she was willing or not.

She screeched her displeasure loud enough to be heard for a mile or more. Hissing, she came to her feet, ready to do battle for her virtue. She was promised to another. Her back hunched and her hair stood up as she backed up cautiously, taking swipes with her sharp claws, snapping with her small but sharp teeth at any who dared to reach for her.

A large cat emerged from the forest, and as he entered the circle, he growled his warning to all the other cats. They quickly dispersed, not wanting to anger their leader.

Cearul looked at Seitka with lust in his eyes. He quickly turned, holding out his hand to her.

Against her better judgment, she, too, turned, slapping his hand away.

"Why do you and yours chase me?" she angrily asked, anger shining in her eyes. She was, after all, the leader of their pack's sister. "Colin will not be happy you have chased and harassed his sister."

Cearul laughed. "You are in heat, little healer. I know of you, and I am not afraid of your brother. Colin means little chieftain, and so he is. I am much stronger and a better chieftain. You will be mine."

"I am promised to Daniel; you know this. He will kill you if you touch me."

Again, Cearul laughed as he replied, "I am not afraid of Daniel, either. Come with me willingly or not, but you *will* come with me, and I *will* mate with you, tonight."

Seitka turned to flee, but it was too late. Cearul grabbed her from behind and quickly flung her over his shoulder, carrying her easily to his home. She screamed and beat on his back with her fists. She tried to change back to cat form, but he had her legs, making it impossible, He was so big and she was so small that it was no match.

He kicked in the door to his hut and, with an evil growl, sent everyone out. He took her straight to his bedroom and tossed her on the bed. Seitka scrambled to get off of it to run, but he was on top of her immediately. Grabbing her wrists, he tied her tightly to the bed frame. While she was tied, it was impossible for her to change.

He laughed evilly before he began to tease her nipples, gently suckling and then pulling them with his teeth. He could smell her heat; it crazed his senses, driving him on. He worked his way slowly down her body, putting first one and then two fingers into her pussy, stretching her. He could feel her body betraying her, feel her tightening inside. He knew she had no idea what was happening to her. His lust grew to a fiery pitch. His hatred of the Tabby Clan and his lust combined to seal her doom.

She was fighting for control, to save her pride and her dignity. She was promised to Daniel. But it was a losing battle. She was in heat, and she had very little control over her body. It responded to the wonderful things he was doing, and he knew it. Her body twisted and squirmed trying to ease the tension; it begged for something. She didn't know what, but she needed it, whatever it was. She screamed in frustration, angry with herself and hating Cearul for doing this to her. Ashamed that her body was reacting, and she could do nothing to stop it, that she was betraying a man she had loved since childhood. She was tied and helpless to make Cearul stop.

He continued tormenting her until she cried in sorrow for what she was about to lose. He rubbed her clit and then circled it, her juices making his fingers slick. He rubbed faster and harder, smiling down at her as he watched her eyes, quickly sending her over the top. She came apart, screaming as he laughed.

"You are a slut; Daniel will be happy to know before he marries you." He continued teasing her body, bringing her to a climax over and over until she couldn't fight anymore. He roughly and cruelly entered her, making sure he put his kit in her belly, with no thought now to her pleasure, only his. His revenge was sweet. She would carry his kit.

She was so ashamed of her body and her actions. She had betrayed her intended and would carry another's kitten. Daniel would banish her, and her brother would be so disappointed. If only she had listened to him.

Cearul was cruelly laughing at her and the shame she felt. "Now, little wild cat, you will marry me, and we will take over your clan. I will rule both clans with an iron paw. Think of all the power I will have."

Sobbing uncontrollably, Seitka managed to scream out her misery. A long, soulful, agonized animal screech, the pain in her voice evident.

The other cats in the tribe had changed before they returned, and they sadly shook their heads. The females pitied her.

"No, I will never marry you; let me go." She struggled mightily, but the ropes were too tight.

Again, Cearul laughed cruelly. "Don't you know, little spitfire, the more you cry and fight, the more I love it." With that, he back-handed her and began her beating. He beat her mercilessly until she fell unconscious.

Late into the night, when all the men had left to hunt, a small woman entered the bedroom quietly.

Seitka was just waking, moaning at the pain throughout her body.

"Shh, little one. Don't wake anyone. Shh." The woman untied her hands and helped her sit up, giving her something to drink. "It is willow bark tea. You must drink it, so you can run. The men have just left; you will have time to make it home if you hurry. They will not return until dawn. Please be as quiet as you can. If Cearul finds out it is I who let you go, he will kill me."

Seitka turned to the young woman, her voice raspy as she said, "Come with me; I will see you protected."

The woman looked at Seitka with hope in her eyes. "Really, you will take me with you? I promise I will do whatever you ask. I will help you escape, but we must hurry and be very quiet. I know where the men are going hunting. Quickly now, turn, so you heal faster and we can move quicker."

"What is your name?" Seitka whispered as she stiffly moved off the bed, swallowing the moan that threatened. She was in terrible pain from the beating.

"Aibreann. I was born in April, you see. Now, let us go. I will go out first to make absolutely sure everyone is asleep or gone. I will let you know when it is safe for you to follow."

Aibreann silently opened the door. Seeing nothing but darkness, she signaled to Seitka. She changed, as did Seitka, and away they scampered out of the village into the forest, headed toward home.

∾

COLIN

Colin had become the chieftain of the village at a very young age. Their father was killed in a fight, leaving him to provide for his mother and Seitka. Their mother followed their father soon after. The love of her life was gone when he passed, and she had no will to live. Colin then brought in a housekeeper, a woman in her mid-forties, to watch over Seitka and help her learn to be a woman and to keep the home.

Ciara was a Godsend for the young chieftain. Being shapeshifters, they didn't do a lot of cooking, but they had to keep up appearances in order to keep their secret. Colin entertained occasionally and was respected by all the villagers, whether they were of his clan or not. He was admired by all his neighbors and friends. All of Colin's clan of shapeshifters were valued and well liked by everyone in the village, also. It was a matter of safety for all the clan to blend in with the humans and to not let their secret be known. Colin had worked hard and, along with the rest of the clan, had plenty of money and was held in high regard. The clan shared in the wealth and prosperity. Colin made sure no one in the clan went without necessities. The handicapped and elderly were taken care of. The widows and children had food and clothing and warmth. Everyone was educated and found a profession as they grew up.

Ciara had reminded Colin that when Seitka turned eighteen, she would go into heat and would need to be protected. Ciara had already talked to Seitka about what to expect and the dangers.

If Colin had a weakness, it was his beautiful sister. She was the opposite of him. He was big and muscled, while she was small and sleek. He was respected for his authority, and she was always a little mischievous. Where his fur was rough, hers was smooth as silk. She was next in line to be the leader, unless Colin married and had a son. The problem was everyone knew Colin doted on his sister and spoiled her. Colin knew his sister wanted to become a healer, and he indulged her. Letting the village healer instruct her, Seitka became a very good healer of the animals as well as humans. She was very intelligent, but she had a soft heart. The death of an infant would cause her to mourn for days. The death of an animal would make her cry every time. If any in the village had a need, she would bring it to her brother. Everyone knew they could give her a sob story and she would give them all her money. She would give away her mittens or scarf in the winter, even though she knew she would be frozen or risk frostbite by the time she got home. She was too innocent and trusting.

Colin knew she would not make a good leader. She just would not be capable of making the hard decisions that had to be made from time to time. He had discussed this with Seitka, and she agreed to marry Daniel.

Daniel had been his best friend and his second in command for years. He was very intelligent and strong. He would make a very good leader. He was firm but fair in all things.

Colin knew Daniel didn't love Seitka, but he hoped it would grow. He knew Seitka loved Daniel, long ago. She followed them around when she was very young, inviting a scolding from Daniel just for the attention. How many times had Daniel looked at him in frustration?

Colin also had visions of the future in his dreams. His dreams had saved the lives of himself and his clan, many times.

Ciara saw the signs of Seitka's "coming out" days before Colin noticed. She was a little higher strung than normal, itchy, short tempered, not her usual sweet-tempered self.

Colin had instructed her to stay inside in order to protect her. He should have known his sister would not take well to instructions. She never did. She always fought having to obey.

She demanded to be let out, so she could wander through the forest for herbs she needed for the children who had colds. For once, he put his foot down and, in his most authoritative voice, commanded her to stay inside.

DEFIANCE

*a*fter Colin left with Daniel to hunt and Ciara had gone for a small run, Seitka stealthily left the village to go into the forest looking for herbs and plants to help her patients.

When Colin and Daniel returned to find her gone, there was no note telling them where she was. She was just gone.

"You should have paddled her arse long ago, brother," Daniel declared, disgusted at the lack of control Colin had over his sister.

Colin replied, "You are right, brother, but I didn't have the heart. We'll see how you fare when you are wed and it's time for you to take a stand. Those beautiful brown eyes full of tears will undo you, too. Now, let us change back and track her down. I need to make sure she is safe."

"I can smell she is in heat, Colin. I am not sure I will be able to resist her if I find her alone. You will have to stay with me to keep her safe. Damn good thing our wedding is soon."

Both men changed and left to hunt Colin's sister. She was easy to track because she was in deep heat. Her scent was all through the forest. It wasn't long, and they found where she had changed to cat and taken to the trees—where she had struggled with a group of wildcats. Colin became very worried, along with Daniel.

"Hurry, Colin, I think she is in grave danger. This trail leads to Cearul's village. If he has touched her, I will kill him."

Colin agreed, and both began to run at great speed. When they arrived, they had quietly hidden in the trees just outside the village, waiting for darkness to fall. There were too many men and guards, so they would have to wait until after dark, when the men would go out hunting. It would be suicide to try and take them all with just the two of them. Both men had to force themselves to wait. They didn't hear anything unusual until just after dark, when both men heard Seitka's cry of anguish, her scream of pain.

Colin turned to Daniel with tears in his eyes. They both knew what the scream meant. Daniel wiped the tears from his own eyes as he started for the home of Cearul. Murder and hatred were in his eyes. He would kill the cat.

Colin stopped him, "Stop, Daniel, we will wait a few minutes more. When everyone is asleep, we will get her. It will do none of us any good to get killed. The deed is done; we will help her when we get her home."

When they saw the male cats go out for the hunt, an hour later, and the rest go to their homes, the two men who were more like brothers than if by blood quietly snuck to the edge of the forest. They were just in time to see a young woman helping Seitka out of the house and right in their direction.

Daniel jumped from the trees. Standing in front of them, he looked the women over. Seitka could barely walk; Aibreann had to keep prodding her to keep her moving. Both men turned so they could better help Seitka.

Seitka looked up, only to see the two men she was ashamed to look at standing in her path, pity and compassion in their eyes. Seitka turned, not wanting to look at either of the men but needing their help.

Colin lifted her chin and examined his sister. Her eyes were black and blue already. He ran his hands quickly over her ribs as she grimaced in pain.

"Come, Seitka, let's hurry home, so we can take care of you. Turn back, so we can run faster and you can heal quicker."

Seitka nodded and quickly introduced Aibreann, "She helped me escape. She will need safety, Colin."

Colin agreed, and they all turned to hurry home, careful not to hurry so much as to hurt Seitka any more than she already was.

Once they arrived home, Ciara gasped at the sight of Seitka and immediately went into mother mode. Rushing her to her room to look at her, she called out the door, "Get the healer, someone."

Daniel turned to Colin and said, "I have to leave, Colin. I will get the healer. I will not come back for a few days. I need to think what this means for us. I can smell Cearul on her. She will carry his kit."

Colin replied, "If you no longer want Seitka, I will not force you to marry her. I will not condemn my sister into a marriage where she has no chance of love."

"I understand, Colin, and to be honest, I don't know how I feel. She will have that bastard's kit. I could live with the rape. Having his child is different; he is of the black Irish wildcats. We are the tabbies. That child will have mixed blood. He could become the chieftain someday. The kit will look like the bastard who raped her. I have to know I will be able to be a good father to her kit."

"I had a vision that Seitka would bring peace to *all* the wildcats in Ireland and bring prosperity to us all. I didn't know this was how it would be, but I saw all cats happy and healthy and safe—tabby and black. You could be bringing up the leader of all the wildcats of Ireland, and you would have the honor of calling it son or daughter. If you have any doubts you could love them both, I understand. All I ask is that you be truthful to me and my family, and I will not fault you for it, either way. Think hard, brother, much depends on you being honest with yourself, and you must be very sure. I will not have Seitka hurt."

Daniel nodded and went to retrieve the healer before he left for a few days to think.

DANIEL

After Daniel delivered the healer, he went home to pack a few things for a trip of a week or two. He needed time to think and make sure he was making the right choice for both himself and Seitka and the babe she would soon be carrying. On his way out, he made sure the rest of the clan knew what had happened and he assigned plenty of guards. Colin was only thinking of Seitka, but Daniel knew Cearul would return, not only for Seitka and his kit but for Aibreann, also. He wanted the guards to be very vigilant. Cearul would know Seitka would carry his kit, and he knew the implications. Either his son or daughter could very possibly be the leader of the tabbies and possibly take the black wildcats from him. He knew his hold on his clan was from fear and not respect, and he resented what Colin had built through respect. His hold on his clan was tenuous most of the time. Cearul would have to take Seitka back with him as his child would give him a stronger hold on his clan. She and her kit would be a threat any other way.

Daniel didn't know if he could look at Cearul's kit and not remember what treachery his father was capable of. When he thought of what his precious Seitka had gone through, his heart hurt. He knew he loved her, but he didn't know if he was man enough to live with another man's son or daughter—another breed on top of it. It would taint the bloodline. He stopped when the thought of loving her came to his mind. When had it happened? One minute, he was so frustrated with her, and the next, she was grown up. He shook his head. How could it have taken so long to finally admit he loved her? He thought back on his life.

His parents had been killed when he was a kit, himself. Colin's parents had taken him in and raised him, alongside of Colin. They loved him as their own. He knew blended families could work, because they were as close as brothers. Daniel knew Colin would not blame him, would not take his position away or punish him in any way. But Daniel knew Colin would grow to hate him if he hurt Seitka. He had to be very sure of his feelings.

Daniel thought back to when Seitka was a child/kit. He thought of all the mischief she had gotten into. Colin would scold her, from time to time, but Daniel's hand itched to connect with her cute little bottom more than once. He thought of how happy she was most of the time, her dark brown eyes sparkling with glee when she was happy. They would glisten with tears when she was sad. He thought of the look of emptiness and shame when they had brought her home. His protective instincts were almost choking him. He wanted to make it better, to hold her and tell her it would all be all right, but he couldn't. Not yet. He had to be very sure. Colin had said he had a vision of *all* Irish wildcats living in happy harmony, working together and playing together, at peace with each other. Seitka would be what brought peace among them. Wasn't that worth fighting for? As long as he had Seitka, he could love this child. The babe was innocent of any wrong doing, but what if he or she looked just like its father? Could he live with the reminder all the rest of their lives without feeling resentment toward an innocent child. He thought he was a bigger man or cat than that. Daniel was tired and his head hurt, so he decided to stop, even though he wasn't very far from home yet. He stabled his horse and paid the owner of the hotel for a room, food, a pint of ale and a bath. The maid brought his food and drink to his room as the boys brought in the metal tub and hot water. He ate, then he undressed and sat in the hot tub with his ale, relaxing. He would sleep on this problem and think more about it, tomorrow. He belted his robe, and the boys came to take the bath away. As they took the last of it from his room, a very pretty woman entered his room. She was obviously a prostitute, looking for a little money. Daniel could have pretty much any woman he wanted; he had never resorted to paying for sex. A little voice in his head said it would pay Seitka back for her

disobedience, for putting herself and all of them in this predica-
ment, but as soon as the thought entered his head, he chased it
away. She had suffered enough. This decision had no room for
accusations. They were in this together—all of them. He chased
the prostitute away with a warning not to come back. Falling
onto the bed after locking the door, he slept a restless sleep, full
of dreams of Seitka.

The next day, Daniel rode further towards the edge of the
forest. The forest that surrounded them was huge, covering miles
of the Irish countryside before it opened to the great fields of the
farmers. He was no closer to an answer, but he worried about
leaving the clan alone to face Cearul and his clan. He decided he
would camp out this night and return home in the morning. If he
still had no answer, he would think on it some more. He could not,
in good conscience, leave his clan without his added protection. He
rode on until dark and made camp. The stars were all out, and the
moon was full. The air was crisp, a sign that fall was here and
winter would not be far behind. This made him think of the kit his
Seitka would have in the spring. Shapeshifters didn't carry their
young for nine months. Instead, they carried for seven months. She
would have the child in April. Shapeshifters also aged twice as fast
as humans until they became five years or so. At the age of five
human years, they began to age normally, which left the child at ten
years instead of five. He laughed, remembering the first time Seitka
had changed. She was a year old and it scared her so badly, Colin
had to help her change back. She cried for hours, thinking she had
no control, until her mother explained the way of the wild cat. She
taught Seitka to change back and forth at will before Colin and
Seitka lost her. Even at that age, they still didn't have total control
over the change. Fear might bring on an involuntary change or
sometimes great anger. Seitka was very spoiled, and during a
temper tantrum, she would change back and forth at a rapid rate.
Looking hilarious to an observer, it would only serve to make her
madder and made the change come more and more. Daniel laughed

until tears rolled down his face. The older she became, the more control she had and less fun she was.

He suddenly felt the need for a run. He was glad he was in the forest instead of another inn. He loved the open spaces and being in the forest. He loved the smells and sounds. He quickly changed to his cat form and went for a run, hunting for his food. He ran for miles, catching a small rabbit for supper. His muscles stretched as his stride grew. Finally, at midnight, he returned to camp to stretch out in cat form to sleep. This time, he slept through the night, at peace with his decision to return home. He would marry Seitka in two weeks. He loved her, and she was his destiny. He would tell Colin of his decision as soon as he returned. He would love her kit as his own, and God willing, they would have more kits of their own.

RUNNING

*S*eitka shut herself in her room and didn't come out to eat. Ciara and Aibreann both tried to entice her with her favorite dishes but to no avail. She just wanted to be left alone in her misery. Daniel had left her, just as she had known he would. He was ashamed of her and no longer wanted to marry her. She couldn't blame him, but he had gone when she needed his support the most. Seitka also knew that Cearul would be coming for her and the kit she would surely carry. She was putting herself and the clan in danger, all because she had disobeyed her brother. Seitka cried bitter tears for the love she had lost and the life she could have had. She had asked for privacy, but when the old, wise healer and dear friend and confidant had come, she had cried on the old woman's shoulders. She explained how she had disobeyed and put the clan in danger and how she had put herself and the baby she carried in danger. She cried harder when she explained that Daniel was ashamed of her and had left so he didn't have to face her.

Darcy was an old woman with connections all over Ireland. She was very wise to the way of men and war. She promised Seitka she would think of an answer and bring her the verdict, tomorrow, when she visited.

The next morning, Seitka came out of her room and had breakfast with her brother and the two women. She quietly picked at her food, not hungry. She looked up to her brother who was getting ready to leave as he did every morning to visit every family in the clan. He made sure everyone had all they needed. Winter would be upon them soon enough. She knew he would be visiting all the men who were guarding their home.

"Do you know when Daniel will return, Colin? Did he say when he would finish his business?"

Colin looked down at his feet, not willing to look her in the eye while he lied to her. "He didn't say when he would return, Seitka. I have given him much to do."

She nodded her understanding, even though her brother hadn't come out and said it—Daniel had left because of her.

Colin walked out the door to the stables, sadness weighing his every step. His heart broke for his sister, but he had his obligations to take care of. The guards needed to be relieved and new ones put in place. His clan needed to be protected. He hoped Daniel would return soon to help with the everyday running of things, and he hoped, for all their sakes, he would put his pride aside and marry Seitka.

Darcy returned in the early afternoon to check on her patient. Ciara asked if Darcy could stay while she and Aibreann went to help one of the other families.

Darcy agreed eagerly as she moved to Seitka's room. As soon as the other women left, Darcy turned to Seitka. "As soon as I returned home, I sent up a smoke signal to the great stag. He came down from the mountain to see me at dawn. When I explained to him what was happening, he agreed to take you to a safe place."

When Seitka shook her head, fear in her eyes, Darcy put her hand on her small shoulders and said, "Fear not, child, he knows of a laird many miles from here who has a wife who cares for the animals. She owes the great stag a favor from years ago. She will see to your safety until the babe is born. It will be a hard ride, but the stag will protect you until you arrive at the McGregor Keep. We must hurry; the stag waits not far from my hut for my signal. Take enough for a long journey but not so much someone will notice. We will tell the guard you are visiting my hut for herbs. You can hunt for food on the way, but the stag asks that you stay in human form as much as possible so as not to upset the wolves that will be guarding you on your journey. If you hurry, you should arrive in a week or so. I have sent out a falcon to Maria to let her know of your arrival. I will leave it up to you and the great stag to explain the danger. I know I will not see you again. I have had a vision. Finally, I will be allowed to join my George."

When she saw tears swimming in Seitka's eyes, she quickly took her in her arms. "Do not cry for me, Seitka. I have loved you like a daughter, but I have missed my George. I am ready to go to him, at last. Be happy for me."

Seitka nodded and looked around her room. She would leave Colin a short note saying she loved him and nothing else. She put it on her pillow, so he would be sure to see it. She gathered a change of clothing and some cold meats and fruit. She was ready for her adventure.

They quickly made their way to the stables, where Seitka picked the strongest and fastest horse, explaining to the stablemen she was going with Darcy for some herbs.

Darcy and Seitka galloped to the hut, and Darcy sent up another smoke signal. Soon, the stag arrived.

Darcy and Seitka bowed in respect for the leader of all the animals. The stag bowed his head slightly, acknowledging their respect as was his due.

Darcy gave Seitka a hug and said, "Be safe until you return. I love you always. Hurry now, before they learn you are missing."

The stag took the lead, and Seitka followed at a good clip through the forest. She noticed wolves running ahead through the forest and eagles overhead. This was a new beginning.

∾

COLIN KNEW something was wrong as soon as he returned home, a few hours later. His worry over his sister caused him to hurry though his duties. It was too quiet in the home the brother and sister shared; his cat senses could detect only a very faint smell of Seitka, and the other two women were also gone. He quickly went to Seitka's room, fear gripping his insides. Deep inside, he knew she was gone, and the guilt almost brought him to his knees. He saw the note on her pillow. Picking it up, he read, *"I love you, Always, Seitka."*

When Daniel entered the home and Seitka's room, he found his brother sitting on the bed with tears in his eyes and the note shaking in his fingers. He gently took it from him and read it. He knew, also, that she had run, and he was to blame. There was no mention of Daniel. No words of love.

Colin lifted his head. "She thought you didn't want her anymore. She thought she was shamed because we failed to protect her. She didn't want to put the clan in danger. She didn't trust us to protect her, because she thought we didn't care for her anymore. My God, Daniel, what have we done? We must find her before Cearul does."

Tears were in Daniel's eyes, too. His heart was broken for the man he loved as a brother and the woman he loved enough to marry, even though she carried another shifter's kit. "I will go to the old healer. You must stay here with the clan. I will let them know the situation. I hope Darcy knows where she has gone. I may be gone for a long while, but be assured I will protect Seitka with my whole being. I came back to tell her I love her and want to marry her still."

Colin nodded. "Send word back as soon as you know she is safe. I will be in my own Hell until I know both of you are safe."

Daniel agreed, and after packing a few things, he took a fresh, fast horse and one of the men and headed to the old healer's hut.

Marvin, the guard he took with him, would take word back to the other guards and Colin.

WHAT DANIEL FOUND when he arrived at Darcy's hut made his blood run cold. The old woman was dead, her throat torn and blood everywhere. Cearul or some of his men must have tried to get information from her and then killed her. Daniel knew she would never tell them anything she knew. She looked to have been beaten savagely before they killed her.

Daniel sent Marvin back with the news and a message for Colin. "Make sure you double the guard around our clan and make sure all the clan is aware of the situation, so they can be prepared for danger. Tell Colin I will let him know when I find Seitka. Go now, hurry and let everyone know what is happening."

Marvin headed back to the village at a gallop.

Daniel could see many footprints around the hut. He looked closer to the forest until he found an unusual set. A large stag had been here earlier, and a horse followed him into the forest. Daniel was a good tracker, and he could smell the faint smell of the woman he loved. He changed form, so he could move faster and be more alert to danger as he followed the stag's tracks.

SEITKA FOLLOWED the stag for miles, never stopping to rest or eat or hunt. Finally, she pulled her horse up near a stream and said to the stag, "We must stop, so the horse can rest and drink and I must find a bush. She blushed slightly. "We won't need to stop again until after dark, when I can change and hunt."

The stag seemed to understand as he walked to the stream and began to drink and graze alongside of her horse. Seitka quickly found a bush not too far away and did her business, hurrying back. She pulled out a piece of dried beef and chewed on it, resting next to the water. Taking a refreshing drink, she finished her snack. Soon enough, her horse nudged her, and she mounted, ready to continue. By sunset, she was exhausted and getting cranky. The stag continued, ignoring her complaining. There was a full moon out that night, so they continued until late into the night before finally stopping. Seitka was tired and hungry and needed to find a bush again. She quickly dismounted and headed to the nearest one. She could hear a wolf howling in the distance, and it made her anxious. No wildcat wanted to go against a wolf. They were so much bigger and so fierce. When she returned, she removed the saddle and bridle from her horse and let him graze and drink from the lake. The stag did the same, watching Seitka as he did so. They didn't dare make a fire, but Seitka could see eyes in the forest all around her.

Suddenly, Seitka saw a huge wolf walking into their camp, with a rabbit hanging from his massive jaws. He looked to the stag that bowed his head in acceptance of the gift. The wolf backed away back into the forest. The stag looked to Seitka, letting her know it was hers to eat. He obviously didn't want her roaming the forest hunting. She quickly turned to her cat form and devoured the rabbit, licking her paws after she finished. The stag didn't seem to care that she stayed in cat form as she slept before they continued their journey a few hours later. The sky was just turning grey with dawn when she felt the buck give her a nudge—her signal to change and begin a new day. She quickly went to the lake and washed, grabbing an apple off the tree before saddling her horse and mounting it.

Day after day, they continued the same way until they reached their destination.

MCGREGOR KEEP

*M*aria sighed a long sigh. How had she come to be in this corner again, awaiting Chance's punishment? Twice in one week, for the same thing. She had been so good this year. Oh, sure, the first couple of years, she had been punished for disobeying many times, but in this last year, she had not been naughty one time all year. She had not felt Chance's hard hand on her bare bottom even one time. Now, in one week, she was in this corner twice. She sighed again. Something was calling her to the forest. She didn't know what, but for some reason, she felt the need to go there. Chance had explained to her that something was killing some of their cattle, by tearing them to pieces with sharp teeth. It couldn't be the wolves; they knew better and protected the clan and the animals. Chance had told her never to go to the forest alone until they caught this animal, whatever it was.

Maria had disobeyed him and put herself in danger. She knew he would never allow that. The first time she had left for the forest, Mark had tattled on her, damn him. This morning, one of the other guards spotted her heading to the forest with a basket for herbs and healing plants. Maria sadly shook her head. She was in for a hard spanking. If only she knew what it was that was calling to her. She had disappointed her loving husband, and that pinched her heart. She sighed again, just as Chance entered their room.

Chance looked at his little wife in the corner, naked and awaiting punishment. She was so beautiful that she took his breath away. He loved her so much, the fear of losing her crippled him sometimes. There had been peace for four long years. Now, suddenly, there was trouble brewing. He could feel it in his bones. He had left strict orders for Maria and their three-year-old son, Dylan, to stay in the compound.

"Do not leave the bailey, stay in the gates!" he had told her.

Sarah, the housekeeper, kept a very close eye on Dylan, and Maria was also very protective of her son. She watched his every move. She had been so good this last year. He would take that into account when he punished her. He hated to be so harsh with her, but she could not be allowed to disobey him. He could not keep her safe if she didn't obey him. He had spanked her with his hand just a few days ago for the same disobedience. Obviously, he hadn't gotten her attention. She didn't take him seriously enough. She would most certainly remember this spanking.

Chance sat on their bed, laying down the paddle. He hated to hurt her but would hate to bury her even more. He wouldn't survive, even for their son.

"Come, Maria, let us talk for a minute before we settle this."

Maria looked over her shoulder before turning to walk to her angry husband, tears in her eyes at his disappointment.

He pulled her in between his knees and onto his lap. "Why, Maria, after all this time, do you feel the need to disobey me, not once but twice?"

Maria looked down at the floor, shame not letting her look her husband in the eye.

Chance was having none of it. Putting his finger under her chin, he lifted her face until she looked him in the eye.

"I told you, last time, Chance, something is calling me to the forest. I don't know why. I can't explain it."

"Did I not make myself clear enough last time, lass? Did I not tell you it was dangerous? There is an animal, or more than one, killing cattle. Did you not understand?"

"I understood, but can you not understand that something is calling me to the forest?"

"I only understand that there is danger in the forest and I love you too much to lose you. I understand you deliberately disobeyed me again, even after I spanked you. Come lie over my knee, lass, let us get this done. You will not be so willing to disobey me again, I guarantee that."

Chance lifted her up and over his knee, putting his other leg over hers to trap her legs so they would not kick. Maria knew this was a very bad sign that this paddling was going to be severe. He put the top of her body over the bed and gave her a pillow to grab onto and to muffle her cries, so Dylan would not hear them and become upset. He adjusted her, so her bottom was right where he wanted it before he quietly announced sentence. "I will give you a warm up, and when you are nice and pink, I will give you twenty with the paddle. Do not ever make me do this again, Maria. I do not enjoy causing you so much pain."

He began with sharp, crisp spanks meant to sting and burn. When Maria began squirming and moaning and her bottom was a nice dark pink, he picked up the paddle. He began her paddling at the crown of her bottom and proceeded down to her sit spots and the back of her thighs. By the end of the first round of five, Maria was begging him to stop. After the second round, she was sobbing and begging him to stop. After the third round of five, she couldn't be understood. Chance stopped and laid the paddle on the bed. He began to gently rub her ruby red bottom. He had not bruised her; that was something he prided himself on. No matter how severe, he would never bruise her.

"Shh, Maria love, just five more to go. Shh, you will upset Dylan."

After she gained a small amount of control of her breathing, he picked up the paddle again. "The last five will be harsh. I want you to always remember to never disobey me again when it comes to your safety. Understand, my little Maria?"

Maria sadly nodded her head and answered, "Yes, Chance, I will never disobey you again and go into the forest alone—until you tell me it's safe. I promise."

Chance picked up the paddle and finished with the hardest spanks she had ever received right on her sit spots, before he lifted her back onto his lap and cradled her in his lap. He was careful to spread his legs, so her bottom didn't touch. He rocked her and crooned to her sweet words of love, until she stopped sobbing and he gently placed her on her tummy. Kissing her head, he covered her. "Sleep, my love, I will wake you in a couple of hours. Please, never make me do this again."

Maria was asleep when Chance left their room and went to find their son. He needed to hold him for a while to make sure all would be right in his world. Dylan was a little replica of his father, with deep blue eyes and dark hair. He was very intelligent for a three-year-old, or so his father thought. He spent the time Maria was asleep teaching his son how to ride his new pony. Rolland had had it sent over, along with the mother, when Dylan became a year old. It was Chance's pleasure to train the colt to carry his son. He loved teaching Dylan to ride. The mother of this colt was Maria's favorite mount and was bred with one of Rolland's Irish draught ponies. Soon, he would have another colt to train.

Mark, his brother and second in command, was training the future laird of the Macintosh clan. Wolf was training the future laird of the MacGyver clan. The boys were fourteen and fifteen, respectively, and coming along very well. Both boys would be ready to return to their clans in a very few years and were growing into fine men. Chance had a feeling Mark was attracted to Chad Macintosh's mother, but he wouldn't admit it. The boys returned home during the fall to help with the harvest and returned to

Chance and Wolf's homes before the snow fell. Chance had heard nothing but good things from Wolf about Timothy MacGyver.

The king had tried and hung both boys' fathers for treason to the crown after the battle of the abbey, four years before. Since then, things had been relatively quiet and peaceful.

Just as Chance returned, his son on his shoulders, a falcon landed. Dylan squealed at the falcons when they landed not far ahead of them. Squirming to get down, Chance knelt on the ground to allow him to get off. Dylan slowly and carefully walked to the falcon as Chance watched nervously. His son had the same gift with animals as Maria. The falcon waited patiently for the little boy to unfasten the leather strap that held the canister with the note. Dylan was very gentle as he unfastened it. After retrieving the note, he went to hand it to his father.

"Give the falcon a special treat, Dylan." The boy scrambled to the stable, the falcon following.

Chance read the note from Darcy as he remembered stories of the old healer.

"I have a special woman coming with the white stag. She needs protection. Please help her. Darcy."

Chance waited for his son to return before he left him with Sarah. He climbed the stairs to his room and bent over his still sleeping wife. "Maria, little one, it is time to awaken." He kissed her temple.

Maria rolled over before she remembered her spanking and squealed. Angrily, she glared at her husband. "Was it necessary to be so harsh, husband?"

"Yes, Maria, it was and will be even worse if you go into the forest again without a guard along. Understand, wife?"

Maria nodded her head. "Yes, husband."

She stretched her arms over her head, letting the covers drop below her breasts.

Chance moaned, "Maria, have mercy on a man."

She just laughed and looked innocently up at him. "Then, why did you wake me?"

"You received a note from a Darcy. Isn't that the old healer who has been around for years? The one who lives on the other side of Ireland?"

Maria nodded. "I have heard rumors about her since I was very little. She is one of the best healers Ireland has ever seen. Very wise, too, if I remember right."

Maria read the note with a serious look on her face. "What can this mean, Chance?"

"It means we will have company soon, so you should be on your best behavior. We will find out what this is about, soon enough. Your old friend, the *Arsa* buck, will be with them, so we will know for sure it is the woman Darcy was talking about. Also, you will meet him in the bailey; you will not go to the forest to meet him. Do you hear me, Maria?"

She nodded again. "This may have been the reason I was drawn to the forest."

"Or," Chance continued for her, "it may be the animal that is tearing our cattle apart. Do not test me on this, little girl. Now, young lady, your son misses you and you have much to do to be ready for company. I will let Mark know to be on the lookout for the stag and his companion."

Maria spent the next couple of days readying for company. The guest room was cleaned, and Mark and Chad kept a careful eye out for the stag while guards looked further into the forest. Another steer had been found dead, and this worried Chance. He had Maria "talk" to the wolves to let them know to kill anything they saw that was killing the cattle. Maria also sent a note to Wolf to let him know of the killings, in case he started having the same problem. Chance wanted to give Wolf the heads up, so he could keep his family safe. Pup was six-years-old now, but Caitlin was only three, and he knew Amanda was a handful. He knew Wolf would send the message on to the rest of the lairds. Rolland's little girl, Ava, Wolf's daughter, Caitlin, and Dylan were all pretty much the same age, born in the same year. They all met at the abbey every year to celebrate the birthdays. Chance smiled when he thought of the battle of the abbey. It was four years ago, now. It still made a hell of a story. Six lairds and their families now protected the healers. The king had wanted to bring the clans together and make a pact with England. His Majesty had offered his beloved goddaughter to Wolf, the fiercest but also the fairest among them. Amanda was trained in many countries by the wisest healers the king could find. Each of the lairds contributed a healer to Amanda to train and then return to their clans. The healers had all married and had families of their own by now.

Wolf and Amanda had Wolf, Jr. (Pup) and Caitlin. Rolland and Colleen had Danny and Ava. Samuel married Kary, but they had no children as of yet. Acelin married Hope, the niece of Erich, and they had a son, Ardan. Jamie, the son of Isaac, married Kelly and had a son, Sean. He, himself, had married Maria, and they had Dylan.

Each of these girls had their own special gifts besides healing. Amanda was a wonderful teacher and organizer. Colleen was a seer as well as a healer. Hope was psychic and a seer, as well as needing to be a little one, from time to time. She was also deaf.

Maria had a close bond with animals. She could make them understand what she wanted. She understood them better than humans, many times.

All the lairds had a bond, not just because their wives were the king's healers protected by the crown. An amulet around each of their necks proclaimed them to be protected by the king, himself, and warning of dire punishments, if anyone harmed one of his healers. These little healers tended to find themselves over their husbands' knees for disobedience, most of the time putting themselves in danger. This was something no laird would tolerate from anyone in the clan, much less the woman they loved more than life, itself.

Dylan scared the kilt off him, sometimes, as their son had inherited the gift of his mother.

At three-years-old, he could call the falcons and the pigeons. The wolves walked right up to him to be petted. Wild animals all loved him, and Dylan thought nothing of it, as if it was as natural as breathing.

Chance shook his head in dismay, dismissing the picture he had conjured up in his head. He would be grey at a very early age, at this rate.

A GUEST

*S*uddenly, Mark and Chad came galloping into the bailey. Jumping from his horse, Chad ran to Chance shouting, "The falcons are circling. Someone is riding in hard and fast."

Mark smiled at the boy he was beginning to love like a son. He was used to the falcons letting them know when someone was arriving, but Chad never got over the awe of it.

He put his hand on Chad's shoulder and suggested, "Let's ride out to meet them and bring them into the bailey where it's safe."

Chad nodded excitedly, and they mounted and galloped off to greet the guests. Mark couldn't wait to see Chad's face when he met the ancient stag. He, himself, had only seen him on one occasion, and he had been truly humbled.

Chance went to find his wife to let her know their guests had arrived. No doubt, she would want to ride off on the great stag and come to an understanding about the guest. Again, Chance shook his head. He knew the eagles and wolves ran with him and Maria would be perfectly safe, but he had to give up control of her safety and that thought turned his stomach. He would have Sarah help him with Dylan. Lord only knew the child would want to go with his mother.

"Take him to the kitchen for a treat and keep him there," he instructed the housekeeper he trusted with his son.

"Aye, Laird, but he will be angry if he misses all the excitement." The old woman shook her head and went inside to find the boy.

The eagles, falcons, and wolves all poured into the bailey. Behind them, Mark and an awestruck Chad rode. Following, as fitting for a regal beast, the ancient stag and a very young woman on a horse.

Chance and Maria stood side by side at the door of the keep. As the procession stopped and the great stag stepped forward, both Chance and Maria bowed. The revered animal nodded his head as his due. Maria tried to take a step forward, but Chance held her tightly.

"Maria, please, you know how this part terrifies me."

Maria just smiled as she pulled her hand free and went to welcome the young woman.

"I am Maria, and this is the laird, my husband, Chance." She turned to Chance who stepped forward with his wife.

"It is my pleasure to welcome you to our keep. Please come in and take refreshment. Maria has seen to your room, also, so you may rest before we talk."

Just as Maria was walking over to the stag, Dylan came bursting out of the keep, skidding to a halt when he saw his mother touching the stag. Mark and Chance ran to stop the boy before he took off to his mother, but they were too late. Sarah came running out, looking wildly for the child when she saw him run to his mam.

She looked to Chance, tears forming in her old eyes, and Chance patted her on the back. "Please, Sarah, will you see to this young woman? We will see to Dylan."

By the time Chance slowly and carefully walked up to the great stag, Maria had the boy on her hip. He was petting the stag on his nose and the animal was allowing it. The boy was chattering away to the stag as he petted him. Maria watched with a huge smile on her face.

"The stag and I must come to an agreement about the girl. He must explain what it is he wants from us. I must go with him."

"Give me the boy and you may go, but, Maria, you tell him about the beast that is killing our cattle. And make sure he knows if he allows anything to happen to you, wolves or no wolves, I *will* hunt him down."

The stag nodded his head and lowered himself so Maria could climb on his back. Dylan screamed and held out his arms to his mam, squealing and squirming and crying out.

Maria looked at Chance. "Please, Chance, let the child come with us. He will come to no harm, I promise. We will hurry back to you, so you don't worry. Please, husband, it is his gift, also."

Chance did not want this at all. He slowly shook his head, his fear showing in his eyes. Terror gripped him as he clutched his son. "Not both of you, Maria. I will not survive if I lose you both."

Maria smiled, and the great one rose, his nostrils flaring in anger. Stomping his foot, he nudged the arm holding the child.

Maria held out her arms for her son. "Do not worry so, Chance; please, we are safe."

Chance knew he had no choice, really. He slowly handed his son to his mother. Looking at the great stag, he shook his finger in his face. Too full of fear to speak, he turned to stomp off.

The great stag took Maria and her son out to the forest. They returned in an hour, and he left to stay in the forest until he was called, the eagles and wolves again following their leader.

Chance had sent everyone away to their duties as he sat on the bench at the entrance of the keep waiting anxiously, fear consuming him as he watched for the falcons to return. As soon as the great stag entered the compound, he rose and ran to his family, his very reason for living. Raising his arms for his son, Maria handed him down to his father as the great stag knelt for Maria to get down. The stag bowed again and walked regally to the forest.

"He has given instructions to his wolves, as well as ours, to be on the lookout for whatever is killing the cattle," Maria explained.

Chance nodded in acceptance before tossing his squealing son into the air and giving him a huge hug, until Dylan squirmed to be let loose and down.

I talked to the *Arsa,* Da. I told him how old I was and how I liked riding with him in the forest. He understands me, Da. I really like him, Da," the child prattled on all the way into the house.

Chance and Maria listened to him solemnly, knowing this was his gift as well as his mother's.

Sarah ran to the family she had served since Chance and Mark were boys. "Dylan, come with me, child. I have molasses cookies for you in the kitchen." She turned to Chance and Maria and added, "I have put Seitka in the guest room at the end of the hall. I thought you would still want some privacy of your own. I let her know supper will be at six. You still have time for a little…um…nap." The old woman winked at the couple before leaving with their son.

Chance scooped up his wife and headed up the stairs to their room. "That old woman gets cheekier every day, I swear. Come, wife, I need to feel you and know you are safe."

Maria sighed, "Yes, husband, I need to feel you, too."

Inside their room, Chance lowered his wife slowly to the floor, taking her lips on the way down. Maria wrapped her arms around his middle, pulling him closer. He broke the kiss and continued to look into her eyes, a hungry smile on his face as he slowly removed her clothes. When she was finally naked, he quickly began removing his own.

Maria pulled back the covers and lay on the bed, raising her arms in invitation.

Chance quickly entered the bed and pulled his wife into his strong, safe arms. He nuzzled her neck, nipping at the spot between her shoulder and her neck, raising himself up to kiss her again; this time, a hot sizzling kiss.

Maria's hands roamed over Chance's strong back, holding him close. "Husband, let me pleasure you first, this time. I need to make up to you the worry you endured. Needlessly, I may remind you, but I know you were very uncomfortable while we were gone. Allow me to make it up to you. "

Chance rolled over, letting Maria on top as he gently played with her breasts. She threw her head back as she allowed him his play.

She lowered herself until her mouth was even with his cock. Teasing him, her long braid brushed against the muscles on his stomach. She licked her lips to ready herself. Her husband was very large. She lowered herself until she could take him in her mouth, her hands gently cupping his balls. She began sucking in and out, her tongue twirling around the head every now and then. More and more, she took of him until he moaned and rolled. She continued enjoying the power it gave her. She had the power to bring her big, strong husband to his knees if she so desired.

Chance moaned, and holding her head still, he drove his hips up and down, forcing his cock deep into her mouth until he came close to losing control.

"Enough, Maria, I will not be able to wait for you." He rolled her onto her back and began suckling her breasts. His breath was coming in pants. He went down further until he was between her legs. Spreading them wide around his shoulders, he began sucking gently on her clit.

Maria squealed and then moaned. Her lips parted as her breathing became ragged, and her hands caught in his hair as he continued, finally coming back up to her breasts. She could feel the tension building, her muscles tightening, just as Chance entered her, pushing his cock in to the hilt. Maria tossed her head, moaning, "Oh, God, Chance finish it, pleeeeese!"

Chance just grunted as he pounded into her, until they both shattered, coming apart in each other's arms. Their breath came in large gulps as Chance carefully rolled off his little wife. Minutes later, he left the bed, going for the pan of water left off to the side of the fireplace. The fire being banked low, it made the water nice and warm. He walked to his wife, kissing her forehead before he began to gently wash her and then himself. He returned to the bed and pulled her close, her head over his heart. Maria fell asleep in his arms to the sound of his strong heartbeat.

~

THE COUPLE AWOKE JUST in time to dress for supper.

Maria, stretching her arms over her head, rolled towards her husband. She snuggled back into his arms.

"I should tell you what the stag and I decided, with your approval, of course."

"Of course, wife, continue."

"Seitka is a shapeshifter. She can become an Irish wildcat when she chooses. She is a tabby wildcat." She held up her hand for patience when Chance began to move.

"Please let me finish, and I will answer all of your questions."

Chance stilled, waiting for her explanation.

"There are two types of clans. The black wildcats and the tabbies. Both are rare. The black wildcats can shape shift, also, but are led by a cruel and controlling leader, Cearul. Her brother is the leader of the tabbies. The tabbies have taken the time to blend in with the humans and have made a name for themselves and gained respect by all. They all enjoy the fruits of their labor and have gained much wealth. The black wildcats are led by fear and the clan is afraid of Cearul. The only wealth is had by Cearul and a very few of his leaders. Many of the blacks live in poverty and the women are mistreated, as well as the children. I will let Seitka tell you more, as she knows much more than I do. She was promised to her brother's second and foster brother. Daniel was ready to marry her, when she disobeyed her brother and went into the forest without protection."

Maria looked up into Chance's eyes before she finished. "She disobeyed her brother, and Cearul captured her and raped her."

Chance sat up in bed, taking her with him. Pulling her onto his lap, he said, "My God, Maria, do you not see what could happen to you when you disobey me? That poor girl could have been you." He looked into her eyes, and she saw fear in them.

"I promised not to go into the forest again without a guard, Chance, and I won't. This has brought home the reality more than a spanking ever could. Now, let me finish. She was in heat. Apparently, female shapeshifters come into heat once a year. They can have sex whenever, just like us, but once a year, the women have no control over their urges for ten days, and they become pregnant when they mate during this time. She is now pregnant with Cearul's kit, and Daniel didn't want her any longer and left her with her brother. She knows she has put her baby and the clan in danger because Cearul will come for the baby, if for no other reason than to hang on to power. The baby is part tabby and part black. He could, with this kit, take over both clans."

Chance took a few minutes to think this through before he looked into Maria's eyes. "This can put our clan in danger, also, because she is here. Maybe this is why our cattle are being torn apart."

"That is why the stag and I needed to talk and decide. We all owe the stag a great favor for helping us during the battle of the abbey, but to put our clan in danger is something you, as laird, have to decide. Maybe we can have a meeting of the families in a couple of days, here at the keep, with all of the clan, to let them know what is going on and to ask if they are willing to help."

Chance listened carefully to what Maria had to say before he answered, "The clan meeting is a good idea. I will ask Mark and Chad to spread the word to everyone and maybe make up some postings to put on some trees or buildings in the village. Meanwhile, I will listen to what Seitka has to say and think on it some more before I decide what to do. I think I have an idea that will work, but I need some more time to think about it. Agreed, little wife?"

Maria nodded and replied, "Now, it's time to greet our guest.

The stag has put out "wolf guards" to watch over our cattle. Maybe they will catch whatever is doing this."

They both got out of bed just in time to hear a knock. Maria dove back under the covers as Chance made sure she was covered before he opened the door.

"Laird, Sarah asked us to bring up the bath water now. We are ready to fill the tub for your bath before supper."

Maria squealed in delight, "I love that old woman; she knows how to make me happy."

Chance smiled indulgently at his wife. "She wasn't always so kind. She tanned my britches and Mark's a time or two when we were growing up. We thought she was the meanest woman alive. We know she only loved us, now, but back then, neither of us thought so."

Maria giggled. "I can't imagine how strong of a woman she had to be to tan either of your britches, but I love her for it, because you have grown to be a man to be proud of, and so has Mark."

Chance shook his head. "My da had a hand in it, too, you realize. He used the strap that hangs in the barn to this very day. We were both terrified of it, and with good reason."

The boys had finished dumping the steamy water into the tub and had just closed the door by then, so Maria raced over, dropping her blanket as she ran. Climbing in first, she beckoned her husband to come to her. "Come, husband, let us enjoy our bath and sup, and then we can talk more to our guest."

TRAITORS

aria was seated on Chance's right and across from Seitka. Further down from Seitka, sat Dylan and Sarah. Mark and Chad sat at Chance's left.

Dylan was very good at eating on his own, but sometimes, he spilled his milk, so Sarah was there to help him if she was needed. Both parents wanted their son at the table with them as this was family time.

Some of the soldiers who weren't married or had no home or were due on guard duty soon ate in the great hall in the back.

The cooks had prepared a special meal in honor of the guest. There was roasted pork, potatoes, vegetables from the garden and apple dumplings made special for her. Everyone enjoyed the great meal. The men's cups were filled with mead and the women's with sweet ale.

Chance began as soon as the table was cleared. He raised his cup and everyone else followed. "To our guest, a toast to long health and happiness." He noticed tears glistening in Seitka's eyes before she sniffed and wiped them. She was born of class; everyone could tell.

"Thank you, I appreciate the hospitality, but I am sure you have many questions for me, so let us get started, shall we? The sooner you know what you face if I stay here, the sooner you can protect yourself. I do not want to put your clan in danger. If you feel I am, please just tell me, and I will have the stag take me somewhere else. To me, the only important thing is my child."

Chance could see that Mark and Chad were listening carefully as he began, "First, I would like to know when this child is due to come into this world, so I know some kind of time line. Also, I would like to know more about shapeshifters. I feel we can better protect ourselves if we know exactly what we are dealing with. Before you start, I would like some privacy. I am not ready to share your story with everyone. Mark, can you see everyone out but the people at this table?

When everyone had left, he began again, "You look like a beautiful young woman. Can you change at will? What are your limitations? Is anyone likely to come looking for you besides this Cearul or his clan?"

Seitka nodded that she understood. She quickly stood and shed her clothes, changing into her animal form. All at the table gasped as the large, sleek cat roamed behind the chairs. Her beautiful stripes accented her eyes and body. Chance and Mark stood as she came closer to Sarah and Dylan.

Dylan got off of his stool before anyone could get to him and walked over to the cat.

"Dylan, stop, get back. Sarah, take him upstairs quickly."

Dylan ignored his father and just walked over to the cat, that rolled onto her back and let the child pet her stomach—a show of submission for any cat, to expose their belly.

Chance was taking no chances, though. He walked carefully to his son and handed him to Sarah, who took him, kicking and yelling, upstairs.

Chance knelt down and petted the cat as Maria, Mark, and Chad gathered around her.

Just then, Seitka changed back into a beautiful woman. As she rose from all fours, Mark quickly wrapped her into his plaid to cover her. She walked back to the table. Suddenly, she turned to the back of the room. In the shadows, sat one of the guards. Seitka sniffed the air before pointing to the man, in his mid-twenties. His black hair and dark startled eyes looked at Seitka.

"He is a black wildcat and the enemy. He is probably the one killing your cattle."

Mark stood to capture the man, but he ran out the door and changed to cat form, running out of the gates before anyone could do anything about him.

Seitka shook her head. "I hope the stag and wolves get him. I did not see anyone following me, but he must be one of Cearul's spies."

"I don't recognize the man," Mark spoke up. "But he could have been here for days already."

Chance nodded that he understood. "He could have been spying on Darcy and learned where I was headed before we left. His spies live in fear of failing Cearul. Cearul has no tolerance for failure. He punishes them or their families severely if they don't come up with results."

Chance looked at Mark. "I don't understand a leader like that. How can he have the people's loyalty? How can he trust they have his back?"

Seitka nodded before she spoke again. "I don't think he *does* have their loyalty, but he has their fear. He keeps his people in poverty to control them. That is why he wants to marry me and claim my child. This child is of us both, both clans, so he thinks it will help him become more powerful if he has the child of the tabbies' leader as well as his. He thinks to become the leader of both the clans. I will never allow him near my child. I would die before I allow him to raise my child. He is cruel to the children and women, along with the rest of his clan."

Chance stood, holding out his hand to his wife. "We bid you a restful night. We'll talk more, in the morning. I will have extra guards, whom I know, watching the door, so you will be safe. Mark, may we see you in the study before we retire? I would have some things to discuss with you."

One of the maids led Seitka to her room, asking if she needed anything before she retired.

Mark, Chad, Maria, and Chance walked into the study, closing the door.

"I would like your opinion on the happenings tonight. Also, I want to spread the word to everyone that we will have a clan meeting in two days' time. Maria and I will make sure everyone knows, even the farmers. I will ask Sarah to see to a meal in the bailey for everyone. I want everyone's opinion and acceptance before we put the clan in any danger, and I want everyone to be aware, so they can protect their families. I am going to ask the stag to keep some of his wolves and eagles for added protection, especially for the farmers who live further away from the keep. Also, I think I have a plan, but please let me know what you think. I value your opinion, brother."

Mark nodded in acceptance. "As I yours, brother."

Maria sat and listened quietly as Chance explained his plan to protect Seitka. "I thought to bring the other lairds into this as they also owe the stag. We could take her to the abbey. There, we can protect her better. We would have the caves, of course, but the abbey is in the middle of all of us. She can have her kit at the abbey, with Hope and Acelin. We were going to go to the abbey, all of us, in the spring anyway, to celebrate all the children's birthdays. It would work out. Hopefully, we can figure something out by then, or the threat will be eliminated."

Mark spoke up, "Maria, can you send out messages to everyone? I will meet them all in one week at the abbey, and we will discuss it. Is that acceptable, Chance?"

"Yes, and take Chad with you. I will expect you to be back in two weeks. I will keep the stag here until you return. Maria, send out an emergency message to all the lairds. We will need to all agree and work together."

Maria agreed, "First thing in the morning. Mark and Chad and a few men can leave. We all know we stand together. That is the agreement we all made at the abbey after the battle."

"I would rather it just be Chad and me, Maria. We can travel faster and quieter, just the two of us. We will take a couple of wolves for protection."

Chance agreed, "Done. Now, let us find our rest as we all have much to do in the morning, Maria, call the stag in the morning, also, and tell him what we need."

"Aye, Laird," she sassed as she seductively walked out of the room. Looking over her shoulder as she reached the door, she added, "Do not be too late before you follow me, husband."

Chance chuckled as Mark shook his head. "You will never tame that one."

"Nor do I want to, brother."

With that, they all went to their rooms for the night.

THE NEXT MORNING, Maria explained the plan to Seitka. She told her about the battle of the abbey and how the great stag gathered all the animals to help save the lairds and all the clans in their part of Ireland. She explained how Chad and Timothy's fathers had planned to take over their clans and break the peace with the king. She talked about the healers and their laird husbands and assured Seitka she would love them all.

"The abbey is in the middle of us all and protected by each clan. It will be the safest place for you. Hope and Acelin will help deliver your baby, and you will be protected. Acelin and Hope are very talented surgeons. You will have the best care, and the nuns and Father Dominic will help to hide you."

Seitka nodded her head in agreement.

"Mark and Chad are going to the abbey to meet with all the lairds now to get their approval."

Chance entered the keep just as the girls finished their talk. "Are you ready, wife? We have quite a bit of travel to do today to inform everyone of the meeting."

Maria reached up to kiss her husband good morn before she turned back to Seitka. "The stag stays to protect you, and the guards have strict orders not to let anyone in. Others are out looking for the traitor who infiltrated our home last night. You will be safe, while we spread the word of the meeting. We will return by supper tonight." She moved to kiss the young girl's cheek.

Seitka walked them to the door as Chance turned to order her to stay in the keep and out of sight. With a sigh, she agreed. She watched as they mounted up and galloped off. She wished she could shift and go for a run, but she knew it was out of the question for the time being.

Seitka spent the morning puttering in the kitchen, making cookies for Dylan to munch on later. Later that afternoon, she followed Sarah upstairs to put Dylan down for his nap. She sat with the little boy, telling him stories of her home and her family. She answered all of his many questions patiently. The child was a wonder. She could feel a closeness to him already. When she had turned the night before and he had come to her, she could hear his thoughts. She was sure he could hear hers, as well. After he fell asleep, she slowly walked to her room. She was so tired, she decided she needed a nap.

Her lower lip trembled as tears formed in her eyes. She struggled to hold back the sob until she reached her room. She lay on the bed and thought of all she had lost because of her disobedience. She had lost her brother and Daniel, the man she had loved most of her life. She had put her unborn child in danger. Loneliness overwhelmed her, and sobs racked her small body as she held her stomach and her unborn child, rocking herself on the bed.

Suddenly, she felt someone sit on her bed and reach over to brush her hair out of her face.

"Shh, little one, everything will work out. Chance will see to it. Never doubt it. Shh, you will make yourself and the babe ill." Sarah rubbed her back until she fell into an exhausted sleep. Sarah had tears in her own eyes as she quietly left Seitka's room.

DYLAN'S GIFT

*W*hen Chance and Maria returned home, Sarah sat them down and talked to them.

"The lass is lonely and afraid. She has lost everything she holds dear. This afternoon, she cried like her heart was broken. I heard her tell Dylan about her home, and I think I know where it is. I have heard of her brother. Can't we send word to them? She needs her family now."

Chance thought for a few moments before he answered, "The villagers will be here in two days' time. We discussed Seitka and the danger. I told them to be on the lookout for any kind of wildcat. I will think on sending word to her brother—maybe after she has left for Wolf's lair. We can talk to him and see how we feel about him before we let him know where she has gone. I will think on it. In the meantime, she is safe here. We await Mark and Chad's return."

Maria stood from the table. "I will get her for supper; she must be hungry. Where is my little man?"

"I sent him with Bric to give his horse an apple. Not that he needs to bond with the animal. All the animals seem to love him."

Maria walked up the stairs to Seitka's room, knocking softly. As

Seitka answered the door, she informed her that supper awaited her.

Seitka wiped her eyes and ran cold water over her face. Smoothing her dress, she lifted her chin and walked to the big room for supper. She didn't want anyone's pity. She had brought this on herself, and she would have to live with the consequences. She was strong. She could raise her son or daughter on her own.

Chance held out her chair for her as Sarah sat down with Dylan. Dylan wiggled out of his seat and ran to Seitka before Sarah could stop him. He looked into her sad eyes and laid his hand on her arm.

"Do not be sad, Seitka. Don't cry anymore," He looked towards his parents, pointing to them. "We love you and will protect you." Dylan walked back to his seat as dignified as a much older boy, sitting quietly.

Tears began rolling down her face before she could wipe them away. "Thank you, little man. You are truly a wonder. I only hope my little one will be as wise as you when he is your age. His life may depend on it."

The kitchen help began bringing hot bowls of soup and duckling with potatoes to the table. Fresh fruit accompanied it. Seitka ate very little. Her stomach felt unsettled lately.

She pushed her food around on her plate until Chance looked at her and said, "You must eat for the baby, Seitka, as much as you can. Maria had a hard time eating for a while, too, but she drank some of the healer's tea and it helped settle her stomach. I will see to it she makes some for you, too." He smiled a kindly smile.

Just as they were finishing their meal, in rushed one of the guards. "Laird, there is a big man, a warrior, asking to enter and talk to you."

Chance stood with a confused look on his face as Maria and Sarah tried to corral little Dylan. Seitka's eyes grew round as she whispered the name that came to mind, "Daniel." She turned to the guard, an urgent look on her pretty face, fear in her eyes. "Is he big and strong, with long black and brown and grey streaked hair?"

The guard replied, "Yes, ma'am. He has strange hair of many colors, and it is long. The same color as yours. No doubt about him being a warrior, either."

Chance quickly turned to Maria. "Take the child and Seitka upstairs. Do not come down until I call for you."

Maria answered, "No, husband. Sarah, take Dylan and Seitka upstairs. I stand with my husband."

Chance looked at his petite, beautiful wife again and said, "You will pay later for this blatant disobedience, wife. You do understand."

"Aye, I know and would have it no other way, but it is my duty to stand with you, and you know as well as I the stag or wolves would not let anyone come near without knowing no harm would come to us."

The guard quickly spoke up, "The stag is with him."

Maria smiled up at her husband. "I knew he would not let harm come to us."

Chance shook his head as he watched Seitka and Sarah leave with Dylan. They signaled to the guard to allow the visitor to enter.

Chance and Maria watched as, first, the stag walked in, followed by a very large warrior indeed. Chance's first impression was *this man is very dangerous.* Daniel rode in, full of confidence, on a pure black stallion. He was of an impressive size and looked to be a leader.

Seitka peeked out from behind the door. She was joined by Sarah and a wiggling Dylan. The sight of Daniel made her mouth water. Her heart beat faster, and she scolded herself for not remembering he threw her away. He didn't want her. Still, the sight of him riding from the gate with his long hair flowing behind him in the wind, his bare, very muscular chest dusted with a light-colored hair made her want to forget that fact.

His strong, muscular arms held his skittish beast in perfect control as the horse walked up to Chance. He quickly dismounted, showing Seitka his buckskin pants that molded to his strong legs. She licked her lips as he walked to Chance, giving her a view of his tight bottom. She put her hand over her mouth as she kept herself from calling out to him. She was used to obeying him in everything.

As he arrived before Chance, he coldly looked him over. "I have come for my fiancée. Her brother has sent me for her. He is worried about her *safety* and wants her to come home, where we can keep her safe."

Chance was as big as Daniel and a leader as well. He replied sternly, "We are protecting your fiancée. We will continue to keep her safe until we have a chance to figure this out. You may take the message back to her brother. She wishes to stay with us."

"I can smell her nearby." He turned towards the door. "Seitka, come here to me, *now*."

Chance turned towards the door in surprise, mumbling to himself, "Doesn't anyone mind me anymore?"

Maria just smiled.

Seitka slowly left her hiding place, walking toward Chance and Maria. As she stood next to them, Daniel held out his hand to her. "We need to talk, little one, you and I. Come with me, please. I have much to say to you."

Seitka shook her head. "No, Daniel, I will not go anywhere with you. You turned your back on me when I needed you the most. I do not trust you. Tell my brother I am safe with friends. I will take care of myself and my babe." She swore she saw a flash of raw hurt in his beautiful eyes, but it was gone so fast that she thought she must have been mistaken.

Daniel turned to Chance, then. "We need to talk privately."

Chance agreed, just as Sarah lost her tenuous hold on Dylan, who ran out the door and right up to Daniel. As Maria and Chance tried to stop him, he zigzagged out of his parents' reach. Barely coming to Daniel's knees, he poked him in the leg, shouting angrily,

"You made Seitka cry." He gave a shrill whistle that had Maria gasping. The falcons came immediately as the little boy crossed his arms over his chest, an angry look on his face. "I will tell the falcons to hurt you like you hurt Seitka."

Maria quickly ran to her son, looking up at the smiling warrior as he bent and picked up the little boy.

"I love Seitka, young man, I do not want to hurt her. I want to take her home and marry her and protect her. Understand?"

Dylan looked into the warrior's eyes before being satisfied. He looked up to the falcons and gave another shrill whistle that sent them back to the barn. Daniel put the child back on the ground. The great stag looked closely at the child before kneeling in front of him and bowing his head in a show of respect to the boy before turning to leave the way he had come.

Maria looked at them both in wonder, amazement at what had just happened evident in her eyes. Both warriors looked on in awe. Never before had the great stag given reverence to anyone, much less a child.

Seitka stood with her arms crossed as Maria took the child by the hand, leading him back to Sarah, who looked on sheepishly.

Chance said to Seitka and Maria, "Tell the cooks we have a guest for the night." He turned back to Daniel. "Let's go for a ride and talk, man to man."

Daniel nodded in agreement, never taking his eyes off Seitka. Both men turned to retrieve their mounts.

Maria led a very emotional Seitka back into the keep. Sending Sarah to deliver the message to the kitchen staff, she sat Seitka down. Looking into her chocolate brown eyes so full of confusion and sadness, she sighed, "Seitka, do you love this man? Do you trust him with your life?"

Seitka sadly nodded. "I have loved him since I was a small child. I followed him and my brother everywhere. My parents died young, leaving my brother to raise me. Daniel left me when he found out I was raped and pregnant with another's kit. Not just any kit, but a black wildcat's kit. The baby's blood will not be pure. He could not stomach raising a black cat as his own. He did not love me enough, even though he knew I did not ask to be raped. I disobeyed, yes, but I did not ask Cearul to rape me. I could not fight him off. He was too big and strong. He tied me and raped me." Great sobs escaped as Seitka told her tale. Tears made puddles on the floor as she continued. "One of the women in his tribe helped me escape, but it was too late. The deed was done. I was so ashamed. My brother didn't have the heart to tell me that Daniel had left to avoid having to face me and tell me he no longer wanted me. He is a coward, just as I am, for running away. I could not face the shame of being pregnant with Cearul's child. But this child is mine, as well, and I love him or her, already." She laid a hand on her stomach. "I will see him protected. I do not need Daniel and his disappointed looks. How do I know he will not hate the child the day it is born? No! I cannot take the chance. This child must be protected. My brother told me this child has a destiny to bring prosperity to both clans. The black cats are poor and live in poverty, while Cearul and a few have much. This child will bring both clans peace."

Maria had tears in her eyes, also, as she said, "Oh, Seitka, how brave you are. Why don't we see what Chance thinks? Maybe there is hope. Do not give up just yet. Daniel may be a better man than you think. Give it a chance. If, after you think about it and listen to him and what he has to say, you still think you must leave, we will help you. Let us get through the meeting with the clan first before you decide. Agreed?"

Seitka nodded before slowly getting up and starting for the stairs. "I am going to take a nap; I feel so tired lately. Thank you, Maria, for taking me in and protecting me."

Maria heard Seitka's door softly close as her son came running in to her with a cookie in one hand. Maria caught him up and lifted him to her lap. Taking the cookie and setting it on the table, she lifted his face to look at her.

"Young man, where did you learn to call the falcons? You know you are to ask me every single time you do anything with them."

Dylan looked down at his little chubby fingers. "Yes, Mama, I know, but that bad man hurt Seitka. I saw her crying."

"Dylan, you know that is no concern of yours. You are a little boy and don't understand much."

"I know he really loves her. I could feel it in his eyes."

"You mean see it in his eyes, don't you, Dylan?"

"No, Mama, I could feel it. He loves her and misses her, and it hurts him to see her crying. I could tell when I touched him."

Maria looked at her son in wonder. "I'll be damned," she exclaimed.

"I am telling Da you said a bad word, Mama," Dylan chided her.

"You truly are a mixture of us both, young man. If you tell Da, I will tell Sarah no more cookies. Understand?" She held out the cookie for the little boy to take.

Dylan took the cookie, squirming off his mother's lap. Holding out his hand, he shook hers and said, "Deal!"

Dylan took off running to find Sarah and tell her his mama said a bad word.

CHANCE TOOK Daniel to the lake where they could sit and talk. Chance brought two poles and some bait, and both men put their poles in the water before they began.

"Seitka's brother is worried sick about his sister. She left with just a short note. I had gone away for a couple of days. I had to figure out if I could live with her being pregnant with Cearul's kit. It doesn't bother me that the child is a black cat. I am not bigoted and hateful against them. I feel sorry for them, having to put up with the cruel bastard. He starves his people and rapes their daughters. He rules by fear. The tabbies, on the other hand, rule by respect. Our people all prosper. They all respect Colin, because he works alongside of us. He is fair and trustworthy. His sister is the last of his line. She could be the next leader; she is capable, but she has too soft of a heart. Sometimes, being a leader means you have to make hard choices. We were brought up together, and Colin was very happy when I asked for his sister's hand. He knows I will protect her from anything. I will be a good leader, because Colin has trained me to become one. I never thought I would have to decide whether I could live with something like this. It would not be fair to Seitka or the baby if I could not. I would not force her to marry me."

He laughed a sad laugh and went on. "It took me all of one night to realize what a fool I was. It doesn't matter who the father of the baby is. I will love them both. I cannot live without her. I don't blame her for what has happened. I blame no one but Cearul."

Chance got a bite. Standing to land the huge fish, he just shook his head. He took it off the hook and handed it to Daniel, who skillfully gutted it and put it in the shade.

"You have broken her trust, my friend. She thinks you left her when she needed you the most because you didn't love her enough to forgive her. Women think differently than we do. It will not be easy to convince her. I do, however, have a suggestion. We were going to take her to see the rest of our group. There are six of us lairds, all married to healers. We stand with the king for peace between us and England. Amanda is the king's goddaughter, and she is married to Wolf. I have sent a man to the abbey to gather all of us, so we can discuss this. We were going to deliver Seitka to the group and have her stay a month with each clan to get to know all of us and end up at the abbey to birth the babe. We have two surgeons there. She would be in the safest of hands. Why don't you come with us to the abbey? The six of us and the two of you can meet, and you can stay at the abbey until Seitka has the babe. Father Dominic and the nuns will keep your secrets while the clans contribute guards to make sure all at the abbey stay safe. You can get to know us. We can become allies, if that is your wish. We could always use allies."

Daniel quickly stood, pulling in another large fish. This time, Chance grabbed it and cleaned it, adding it to their growing pile.

"There could be a war coming. I can feel it. Cearul wants Seitka and the babe so he can have control of both clans of shapeshifters. He wants to lead them both. I would hate to leave Colin for so long without my help. If anything happens to Colin, I doubt if Seitka would ever forgive herself. We sure could use any allies, but I fear to leave my clan alone for so long."

"What if Colin allowed the great stag and many wolves to help. Would that help?"

Both men stood quickly as both poles jerked once again. They both pulled in two more fish.

"You sure do have good fishing here," Daniel observed, laughing.

"I will send a message to the abbey to ask the men to wait for us to come to them. I can also send a falcon to Colin, and you can tell him you have found Seitka and ask him about the plan. He can send a message back with the falcons. It should take no more than a week. By that time, we should hear back from Wolf and the others at the abbey."

"Is it safe, Chance? Cearul will not get hold of the message, will he?"

Chance just laughed at that. "Maria sees to it the messages go right where they belong. I don't know how, but she talks to the animals in a way only she and the animals understand. Unfortunately, my son has inherited that side of things as you saw. He is too young to know what he is doing, but he shows great promise."

"I think that is a good plan." Daniel rubbed his chin in thought. "It will also give me time to win my Seitka over again. I have a lot to make up for. We will stay for your clan's meeting in two days and spend the rest of the week looking for the traitor, then we can get ready to go to the abbey. Hopefully, we will gain allies and I will gain a wife. The sooner the latter happens, the better for my sanity and for the babe she carries."

"Let's get these fish home in time to cook for supper."

Chance held out his hand to shake on the deal, and Daniel gratefully accepted it.

AN UNDERSTANDING

*A*s the men entered the keep, they could hear laughter. Chance smiled; his Maria had had a hard month. She worried about being called into the forest and had received two spankings for it. As they got closer, they could see the girls playing with one of the new pups. Dylan was helping by lying on the floor and rolling over to show the pup what was required of him.

As soon as they saw the men enter, Seitka excused herself to go to her room before sup. Maria could see Daniel's eyes follow her all the way to her door. Sadness and longing were evident in his dark eyes.

Chance took Maria by the hand and led her to the door as Sarah gathered Dylan to her.

"Dylan is going to help frost the cake for sup tonight. I expect the proper appreciation from everyone."

Maria smiled as the old woman took her son by the hand and led a very happy, excited boy away.

"Maria, I need you to send another message to the abbey, asking for the other lairds to wait for us. We will take these two to the abbey, next week, as soon as Mark returns. In the meantime, we will have our meeting with the clan.

Maria hurried out to do Chance's bidding as Daniel watched.

"It is amazing how she can communicate with the animals," he mused in wonder.

Chance agreed, "She has saved us more than once.

Seitka began to walk downstairs for supper when she was grabbed from behind by Daniel. He turned her to look at him.

"We have to talk, little one. We have much to discuss between us."

Seitka pulled out of his grasp. "We have nothing to say. Your leaving said it all." She continued down the steps to the great table. Maria, the little mischief-maker, had seated them next to one another. As the meal was placed on the table, Daniel served her, putting potatoes, venison, along with the fish, and vegetables on her plate. Everyone chatted about the meeting and what they needed to say to convince the clan that is was worth it to let this couple stay. Dylan chatted with the others about the pups and how their training was coming along. "The runt is coming along, too, Papa. He will grow as strong as the others. I just know it."

Chance chuckled. "I am sure, son, with your care, it will grow to be just as big as the others."

After they had finished the main meal, one of the maids brought in a cake. The frosting was lopsided and looked rather a mess, but Dylan stood, proud as a peacock, and announced he had frosted it. Sarah laughed out loud. "And himself, I might add. I had to give him a bath before supper."

Everyone praised the cake and told Dylan how delicious it looked. They bragged to the young boy about the delicious taste.

Seitka took a small bite. Her tummy was so full, already, but she had to let the lad know everyone loved his cake.

"Oh, my, Dylan, this is the very best cake I have ever had," she cooed.

Dylan smiled proudly all around. "I'll be damned," he proudly announced. Everyone's eyes grew as they looked at the lad, and

Dylan, being very astute, realized he had made a mistake. Trying to fix it, he quickly pointed to his mama. "Mama swore, Da."

Maria looked at her plate, her face red with embarrassment as Chance looked at her. "She did, huh? Well, first of all, you know, Dylan, just because Mama says a bad word does not mean you can. Second, you are not to tattle on others and you know that, don't you?"

Dylan stood, sadly walking over to his mother. "I am sorry, Mama, I tattled on you, and I am sorry I said a bad word."

Maria smiled at the lad. "I am sorry I taught you a bad word, Dylan. Do not ever say it again, agreed?"

Dylan nodded his head solemnly, holding out his hand for his mother to shake. "I agree, Mama, and I am sorry I got you into trouble with Da. I hope he doesn't spank you." He looked at his father. "Don't be angry with Mama, Da. She didn't mean to teach me a bad word. It just fell out."

Maria looked at Chance and the others around the table, her face flaming red with embarrassment.

Chance held out his hand for Maria to take as he gathered Dylan on his lap with the other. "I will forgive mama, this time, since you ask so nicely, Dylan, but only if you never say that word again. As for spanking her, that is private between Mama and me. understand? It's not for you to talk about in front of others."

They all agreed and resumed eating their cake.

MARIA WAS busy introducing Seitka and Daniel to many of the clansmen, some of whom had started coming early that morning. The men offered to help with the butchering and cooking of a pig over a large spit. Many of them brought vegetables to be cooked. The kitchen had been busy for two days baking cakes and puddings for dessert. The cooks gathered potatoes out of the cellars under the kitchen in the keep, and the men were busy hauling up large kegs of mead and two large kegs of some of Aaron's famous whiskey. That would be saved for the end of the day, after an agreement had been reached. Tents were being put up all around, filling the bailey and even outside the great gate. By noon, smells of pork cooking over an open spit and corn on the cob thrown into the coals filled the air. Great tables were all set up and filling quickly with all kinds of breads and cakes. The great stage with chairs was set up in the front, ready for the laird and his family and guests.

Maria was going to put on a show of the falcons, showing how she had trained them to return or to follow them. The wolves stood just inside of the huge forest, guarding everyone. The clan had become used to seeing them and were grateful for their service. Even Dylan was going to show off the tricks he had taught to his puppies, with Bric's help, of course. Bric was Sarah's husband and the stable master. He had taken a great liking to the "little laird" from the time he was very small. He was very protective of him as were all the animals. Bric knew if anyone tried to hurt Dylan, the animals would find that person and kill him or her.

Daniel kept trying to grab for Seitka's hand as they were introduced to everyone Maria could find. Seitka kept pulling her hand away. She had kept her distance from Daniel since he had come. He was beginning to despair of ever mending their rift. Her back was straight and proud as she graciously greeted everyone, her breeding and upbringing evident. She had come from class. Daniel, also, was very courteous and graceful in a different kind of way. He had the way of a leader—confident, intelligent, with a strong handshake for everyone. He didn't put himself above the others in the clan, instead, pitching in to help. The clan noticed his likeness to their own laird. Some of the girls openly flirted with Daniel, but he ignored all but Seitka.

Maria led them from family to family, introducing them and explaining the family tree to them.

Chance was talking to the men of the different families, explaining what he knew of Seitka and Daniel and the plans he had.

He also talked of the protections he had in place to protect their families and farms or businesses.

After the introductions, Maria took the people who were interested to the barns the falcons were kept in. She put on her leather gloves and armbands and called the birds to her, communicating to them to go from her to Seitka, who also stood across the barn with leather gloves and armbands. Daniel stood nearby with a very worried look on his face. The falcons flew to their destination and flew back to Maria. Maria then communicated to them to fly over Dylan, who was in the bailey showing off his training skills with the puppies, mostly to the other children. Dylan laughed when he saw the falcons circling overhead. He knew his mama had sent them to let her know where he was. He whistled to them, and one came down and landed at his little feet. He then whistled again and sent him back to his mother. Everyone stared in awe at the three-year-old.

Daniel walked over to Chance, who had signaled that he was wanted. They went into the keep, where he answered the questions anyone in the clan had. He also took off his clothes and changed to a wildcat, in front of the men. It saved Seitka from having to get naked in front of these strangers, and Daniel was used to being nude in front of others.

THE SPY

"There is one spy out there somewhere who looks like me in animal form but is all black. We need to talk to him, and I suspect he is the one killing your animals. If you see him, send someone to us so we can capture him. In human form, he is much shorter than I am but has black hair."

All the men agreed to keep their eyes open for the intruder.

They all turned when they heard the rattle of a wagon just then, its driver calling to the laird. In the back of the wagon was a cage with a small man with black hair.

"We set a trap for him, Laird, and he walked right into to. We filled the cage with fresh meat. When he entered, I pulled the rope and the door flew shut. We have our traitor."

Daniel and Chance went running, followed by the clansmen. Inside was a wild man, who was fighting to escape. Snarling and hissing, he changed back from cat to human many times. As soon as Daniel walked up to the cage, the animal went crazy trying to pull at the bars, lunging at the locked door.

Daniel calmly began to talk to the animal. "You are Teddy, are you not?"

The animal calmed instantly at Daniel's calm voice. He turned to human and looked up at Daniel.

"Yes, sir, I am Teddy. Please, sir, I have a story to tell. It is important to my family as well as to you."

"Can I trust you not to run? Will you talk to us, so we may figure out how to help you?" The small man nodded sadly.

Chance put his hand over Daniel's and asked, "Are you sure you trust him?"

Daniel looked at Teddy. "Yes, I think he has something he needs to tell us."

Chance nodded to the farmer, who handed the key to Daniel before quickly taking his family back some ways and returning. Daniel opened the doors and quickly tied Teddy's hands together behind him. He then led him back to where they had come from, the keep. All the clansmen followed as the women pointed and whispered but stayed back with their children.

Once in the keep, they all sat at the tables and left the man to stand in front of them.

Daniel waved his hand. "Begin, Teddy, why have you been stalking Seitka?"

Teddy looked Daniel straight in the eyes as he said, "Cearul has my family. If I don't bring at least word of Seitka, he will kill my wife and daughter." Tears filled the proud man's eyes.

Daniel nodded his head. "It is as I thought. This is how Cearul treats his clan. He wants Seitka, so he can control both clans. This, I cannot allow, and Seitka will not stand for this, either."

"Sir, if you could help me get my family back, I will be a loyal servant to your clan. I cannot stay in my clan any longer. My family's safety has to come first."

Chance spoke up with, "Do you know where they are being held?"

Teddy answered, "At a cave near our lands. I know where, but I am only one man, and he has guards at the mouth. My daughter is only three-years-old and the cave is cold. I know the bastards are not feeding them right or giving them blankets. They are scared, and it tears at my heart to think of it."

One of the clansmen stood. "Ask the great stag to send some of the wolves to the cave. Once they have done their work, you can escape with your family."

Chance agreed, "Good idea, Isa. We can get a message for Colin to be waiting for you. He is a good leader, from what I hear."

"Aye, I know it. Unlike our own leader. There are many of us who would like to join your clan but are afraid."

Daniel spoke next, "Maybe you can sneak back in and tell the others that Colin has always been ready to take any black wildcats into the clan. They just must swear allegiance to the clan and keep their paws clean. Even in our clan, Colin has say over justice for the tabbies. He has worked hard to earn our reputation with the humans in our area as being honest and trustworthy. We work hard and share with all the others in the clan. No one is hungry or afraid. He will not tolerate bad behavior or deceit."

"I know. I have heard of your clan. Many of us have, and we envy you. Please, can you help me? I will go back in disguise when Cearul and the guards are gone. I know his habits and schedule. I will tell the others to be patient a little longer. It will give them hope."

Daniel turned to the clan. "What do you wise men think? Shall I take a chance?"

The clan stood and lifted their cups high into the air in a signal they agreed.

Chance asked another question, "Are you agreeable to letting these two stay for a week before we move them?"

Again, all the men lifted their cups high. Chance's heart swelled with pride at the generousness and courage of his clan. "I am proud of you all, clan. Now let's break out the whiskey and have a drink to celebrate a successful meeting before we join the women for supper."

"Before we celebrate, may I impose on Maria one more time to talk to the wolves and to send a message to Colin?"

"Of course; Henry, please ask Maria and Seitka to join us right away, please."

George brought up one of Aaron's barrels of whiskey while they waited for the girls. The men began filling their cups anxiously. Everyone knew of Aaron's whiskey. It was some of the best in Ireland. It was saved for only very special occasions.

DYLAN

he girls walked in with Dylan in tow, and Chance and Daniel filled them in on the plan.

Seitka looked nervously over at Teddy. "Are you sure it is safe to leave him unattended?"

"We have guards watching him. He will sleep in one of the rooms and be locked in until tomorrow, when we send him off."

Seitka nodded her acceptance, turning to listen to a very excited and proud little boy.

"And, Da, you should have seen their faces when the falcons came and, and, and... The puppies behaved just like I taught them. And, and, and... The bagpipes man gave me a piece of candy and, and...I saved it just like you told me. Here it is, Da, can I have it, please?"

Shock showed on Chance's face, mixed with fear. "Let me see it, son, and I will let you know if it is all right for you. Thank you for obeying me."

Everyone watched as the little boy solemnly handed his father his treasure. Chance looked at the candy carefully, smelling and licking it. It had a bitter taste to it, the taste of laudanum. He turned quickly to the guards. "Find this man who plays the bagpipes and bring him here. This is drugged." He turned to Dylan. "You stay here and identify him, son. This candy is poison. I will kill the man who gave this to you."

The rage in his father's eyes scared Dylan and he began to cry, holding out his arms for his mother.

Maria cradled her son, comforting him, "Shh, Dylan, your da is not angry with you, but at the man who tried to hurt you."

Daniel looked at Chance, making sure Maria and the boy could not hear. "Do you think someone meant to kidnap him?"

The pure rage he saw in Chance's eyes frightened even him. "It is the only explanation."

He turned to the clansmen in the keep, men he had known all his life. Men loyal to his da and his da before him.

"If my son is in danger right outside in the bailey, someone in this clan is a traitor, and I will find out who. They will die a painful death."

Every clansman agreed. Chance had been a good laird, his father and grandfather, as well. They would find out who would do this.

One of the clansmen spoke up, "Gary has been bitter since his wife died. He is alone now and not right in the head anymore, but I never thought he would do something like this. He still blames your lady for not saving his wife. We all know she did all she could, but he still holds an unreasonable hate. I think he is not right since Isabell passed this world. 'Tis the only one I can think of."

Many of the others agreed.

Chance turned to another guard. "Find him and bring him here to me."

One of the guards came in dragging a dirty man, with bagpipes dragging behind him, and it was indeed Gary.

Chance lost what little temper he had left. He asked Dylan, "Is he the one who gave you candy, son?"

Dylan nodded his head sadly. "Yes, Da."

"No, no," Gary screamed. "The boy lies. I didn't give him any candy."

Daniel walked over to Chance to quietly whisper in his ear, "The man is deranged and not in his right head, Chance."

All Chance could see was red rage; he had no control at the moment.

Daniel took over. "Put him in the cage this man came in. Let him sit and watch everyone eating while he goes hungry. Drinking while he thirsts, so he understands how good he had it. We will decide, tomorrow, what to do with him." He turned to Chance and quietly encouraged him to go for a ride with him.

"Let us go and burn off some anger, brother. Do not let the clan see you lose control. Some may use it against you someday."

To Maria, he said, "Please see to it the messages are sent."

She quietly nodded her head as she and Seitka took the boy to Sarah in the kitchen. Seitka stayed with Dylan and Sarah, while one of the oldest clansmen drank another cup of whiskey. They knew Chance needed time to calm down.

Daniel and Chance headed out to the hills and rode hard for a time before Daniel halted his horse. They were beginning to lather, and he knew that was not how Chance or he, for that matter, took care of their horses. They looked over the hills, down into the glen, where the waterfall was. The lake was pure and clean and cold. The creek that fed into it was strewn with rocks. Some animals were drinking, not caring that anyone was near. Daniel could feel the wolves behind them. It was amazing how they looked after the clan. "I need a cold dunk in the lake, my friend. Will you join me?"

Chance nodded his head with a grunt, and they began down the hill, the horses carefully picking their way around the rocks. Both men shed their clothes, but Daniel turned to his cat. Chance was amazed at how big this wildcat was. The colors were mixed in his fur. Daniel turned toward Chance before he jumped into the water. Chance followed close behind, and both of them enjoyed a short swim before they got out.

Just as Chance turned to his clothes, Daniel gave a mighty shake, spraying water all over him, huffing and running away as if he wanted to play.

Chance looked at him before he began to dress. "Very funny, cat," he mumbled as Daniel changed back and began to dress with a huge smile on his face. They both took their time getting home.

"This is one of the reasons Colin was afraid to pass the lairdship to Seitka. She hasn't the heart for this."

"I won't kill him, Daniel, but I will banish him. I will have one of the guards give him one last meal before taking him very far away and dropping him off. He will never be allowed to come near the clan again. I don't care if he is not right. He is lucky I let him live at all."

Daniel agreed, "You cannot trust him any longer. You would always be afraid he would stir unrest amongst the others in the clan."

Chance agreed and tried to smile as he entered the keep again, ignoring Gary, who was right out in front watching the festivities. When Chance told the others what the verdict was, a young man stepped up to plead for his father, "Please, Laird, let me take my father to my aunt. She lives on the other end of Ireland. He will never come back, I promise, but my mam's sister will take care of him."

Chance thought for a moment, looking the young man in the eyes, examining his honesty, until he was satisfied. "Very well, but make sure he never comes back. I will allow your family to stay here until you return. I will make sure they are watched over while you take care of your da."

That is why he was respected in his clan; he was fair but just.

"I will get some food for us and begin immediately, and thank you, Laird, for your mercy. He has not been right for some time."

"Bring Dylan here to me, wife."

Dylan was brought back in his mam's arms with a cookie in his hand and all over his face. Daniel and Chance laughed at the sight, along with everyone else.

"Son, thank you for obeying me. You see how easy it would have been to hurt you. That is why we have rules. When I think of what could have happened..." It took Chance a minute to get control of his emotions. "I love you, son." He ruffled the boy's hair before he turned to the other clansmen.

"Thank you for all you do for this clan. I am proud of you all. Now, let us celebrate. Where are the real bagpipes? Let us dance. Come, wife, I need to hold you."

Daniel held out his arm for Seitka, but she turned to leave, ignoring him until Chance took her arm.

A NEW START

"*G*ive this man a chance, Seitka. He deserves a chance to make this up to you."

Seitka looked up at Chance and, seeing his sincerity, nodded her head. Chance had come to really respect Daniel. She could tell by the look in his dark eyes.

She allowed Daniel to lead her outside to the music. She found herself relaxing in his arms and laughing as they did the Irish Jig, clapping their hands to the music and tapping their feet. At the end of the night, Daniel led her to her room. Before she could grasp the knob, he pulled her into his arms, and looking into her beautiful eyes, he lowered his mouth to hers. Gently kissing her, the tip of his tongue tracing her lips, he held her tight as he plundered her mouth.

He lifted her chin with his finger, so she looked him in the eye. "I am so sorry, Seitka. I promise to protect you and love you through any trials we may have if you will marry me. I love you, Seitka, I always have. I just needed a little time to think. I was home within two nights, only to find you gone. Do you know how terrified I was? How hurt your brother was? You could not have faith in our love or in me for just a couple of days? Faith that I would be able to wrap my head around what had happened. Faith your brother would protect you with his dying breath?" He turned her and gave her a swat on her bottom before he opened the door for her.

"You, little Seitka, have something to answer for, also. We will talk more later, but for now, I would like to know if you would go for a run in the forest with me, late tonight, after everyone is settled down and asleep. Does your cat want to run free like mine does?"

Seitka turned to him, her eyes alight with love. "Yes, I would like that very much. Could we go to the waterfall?"

Daniel bowed. "Of course, anything you want." He turned, humming, toward his room as Seitka closed her door with a smile on her face for the first time in weeks.

Later that night, when the house was quiet, Daniel came to Seitka's room. They both undressed and changed to cat before quietly walking down the stairs, the only sound, the clicking of their claws on the wooden steps and floor.

Sarah smiled as she peeked out of her bedroom door.

They walked to the study and climbed out the open window into the bailey, walking out the huge gate after the guard smiled and opened it slightly. With a wave, he called, "I will be waiting for your return."

After they walked a small way away, Daniel began pushing Seitka, nipping playfully at her hind legs, pushing her with his nose. Seitka pushed him back, nipping at his ears. They both began running toward the forest, Daniel in the lead.

It felt so good to stretch her legs. Seitka could smell the musky loam scent of the forest floor. The leaves and pine needles were like the prettiest perfume, the trees so tall and the moon full. They ran full out all around the inside perimeter. She could see the squirrels and owls, hear the crickets and frogs as they came to a stream and stopped to drink. A hapless rabbit ran in front of them and Daniel caught their dinner. While they shared the meat, Seitka looked around. She had missed this—the freedom to run and roam, to feel alive. It felt like it had been years since she felt so carefree. They continued their journey until they reached the waterfall. The lake was so beautiful with the moon shining on the water, the sound of the waterfall not far away.

Daniel waded into the water before he changed back to human. Holding out his hand for Seitka, he encouraged her to join him. She did the same, wading into the water until it was up to her chin, then she changed. The water lapping her breasts, she knelt down.

Daniel lifted her before taking her lips in a sizzling kiss that curled her toes.

"We have much to talk about, but first, I want to know if you have decided to marry me? If so, I would marry you, tomorrow. I love you and want to protect you. Marriage would not only protect you from Cearul but from me, too. I am having a hard time keeping my hands off you."

Seitka looked into his dark eyes, the color of whiskey. She could see no doubt, but she needed to ask, just to be sure, "Daniel, are you sure you can accept this babe?"

Daniel took her chin. "I have thought hard about it and, yes, it is part of you. I will love the babe like my own."

Seitka was satisfied. "Then, I agree to marry you any time you choose."

Daniel smiled as he took her mouth one more time. "Good, then we must talk. First, let me love you, Seitka. It is so painful watching you and not being able to touch you."

Seitka smiled. "I have loved you for so long, Daniel, please show me how to be a woman."

Daniel lowered his head to her breasts, where he took one and gently suckled it and then the other.

Seitka threw her head back, her long hair dragging into the water as a low moan escaped her lips.

Daniel's fingers found her sex, and he inserted one finger and then two, rubbing her rough spot on the inside until he could feel her tighten. He lifted her and carried her to the grassy shore.

Setting her down on all fours, he knelt behind her. His hands roamed over her bottom and then in between her legs.

Seitka wiggled her bottom until Daniel gave her a small slap. It added to the heat building in her pussy.

Daniel placed his cock at her entrance. He could feel she was soaking wet, her juices running down her thighs. He pushed until his cock was just in past the head, and then, with a mighty shove, he was in all the way to the root. He slowly began rocking back and forth, pulling out almost to the end and then all the way in.

"Ah, Seitka, you are so tight, and you feel like liquid heat. I can feel your pussy gripping my cock."

"Please, Daniel, harder, fuck me harder," she moaned.

Suddenly, Daniel stopped. It took every bit of willpower he had, but he needed to say what was in his heart. "You know, if you marry me, Seitka, I will be the man of the family. I will not be like your brother. I will not allow you to put yourself in danger or disobey me or disrespect me. Your brother was far too lenient with you. I will insist on having the last word in any discussions."

"Please, Daniel, just fuck me. Do we need to discuss this now?"

"Yes, little one, I believe we do. Before we marry, I have to hear your promise to obey me in all things. Do I have your promise?"

Seitka squealed in frustration, "Yes, Daniel, I promise, anything, now please *fuck me*!"

That was all he needed to hear before he impaled her on his cock and took her hard. He bit down on the back of her neck and claimed her as only a shapeshifter can. He put his mark on her shoulder for the world to see. *Mine!*

She lifted her bottom to every one of his thrusts, so he could go deeper. He was a big man; he buried himself, filling her all the way to the top, his balls slapping her bottom every time.

Daniel could feel her tightening on his cock. He knew she was close to coming, her moans becoming louder.

"Ah, Daniel, what is happening? I feel something happening, like I want to explode."

"Come, Seitka, come for me now," he demanded, just as she came apart, a loud squeal coming from deep inside her.

Daniel thrust two more times, and he came, squirting streams of his cum deep inside her. He growled as he lifted himself up, walking to the warm water and cupping his hands to collect the water to wash his mate. He let the water run down her bottom into her pussy, before lifting her and walking into the water one more time. He gently used his rough hands to wash her woman parts before he washed himself. He then lifted her and carried her to the grass once more. He lay beside her, pulling her to his chest and brushing her wet hair away from her face before he again spoke, "You promised to obey me in all things, Seitka; you agreed."

Seitka shook her head. "I did, Daniel. I will do my best."

"Seitka, you will always obey me, never put yourself in danger or disrespect me, but most of all, you will never lie to me. If you break any of these rules, I will punish you, and you will not like it. Neither will I."

Seitka lifted her head to look at him. "What do you mean, you will punish me?"

"Seitka, you know what I mean. All the other males spank when they are disobeyed or rules are broken. You know this, but I understand Colin never could bring himself to punish you. He felt so badly for his parentless sister. I, on the other hand, do not have the same problem."

"Daniel, do you mean you will spank me if I break a rule?" She wanted to make sure she understood.

"Oh, yes, every time."

She thought a minute before she shook her head. "No matter. I will not break any of your stupid rules."

"You are disrespecting me right now, Seitka, and you already have a good spanking coming."

Seitka looked shocked. "What do you mean, Daniel? I have not broken a rule yet. How could I? You just told them to me."

"You did not trust enough in our love to give me time to think things through, and you worried your brother to death. You should have seen his sorrow, Seitka. You left him a note, for God's sake. He is your brother, and I was your fiancée."

"I do feel a great deal of guilt, but I have cried myself to sleep because I felt so bad. Does that not count for something? I know Colin will forgive me."

"We have both already forgiven you, but you still need a spanking—to bury the guilt, and then it is truly forgiven and forgotten. We will never talk about it again. Unless, of course, you run away again. In that case, the punishment will be double."

Seitka thought to herself, *how bad can it be? I will get it done and over, and we will be good again. I can do this.*

"All right, Daniel, I will let you spank me but not too hard. "

Daniel laughed at that. "You do not decide how hard or how long or what I use, for that matter. I do! Now, come here to me, Seitka, and let us finish this, so we can run home. The sun will be coming up soon."

Daniel sat on a stump at the edge of the forest, waiting for her.

Seitka slowly walked over to him, looking to him for guidance.

"Right over my knee, Seitka. If you put your hand back to your bottom, squirm, swear, or call names, I will start all over, and believe me, you do not want that. Understood?"

Seitka gulped. "Yes, sir."

That statement had Daniel's cock growing hard again. She leaned over and put herself over his knee, and after he adjusted her and put her where he wanted her, she felt his rough hand rubbing her bottom.

"Tell me, Seitka, why am I spanking you?"

"Because," she began sadly, "I didn't trust you and Colin, and I ran away without talking to either of you first."

With that, Daniel began her spanking. Just enough to sting at first, but by the time he was getting a good start, he had already started a fire. Her bottom began to burn.

"Please, Daniel, enough; it hurts."

"It wouldn't be a deterrent if it didn't, now, would it?" He continued until he heard the first sob.

He lifted her onto his lap and cradled her. "It is done now, little one. You are forgiven, and it is forgotten. We will never bring it up again. Shh, Seitka, it is done. I love you, but please never put me through that again. Shh, little one, let us change and run into the forest again before dawn breaks."

Seitka nodded her head and wiped her eyes. "I don't like being spanked."

Daniel laughed at her. "Then, never break the four simple rules. Easy as that."

Daniel changed, and right behind him, so did Seitka. They both took off running and playing through the forest until they arrived back at the keep. The guard smiled and waved as they walked through the gate and into the study window, only to meet Chance.

He smiled at them both. "The priest will be here shortly, so you had best get some rest before your wedding. Don't you think?"

Both cats climbed the steps and entered Seitka's bedroom before they again changed back to human form. Lying next to Seitka, pulling her into his arms, they both fell asleep, dreaming sweet dreams.

Later that afternoon, there was a knock on the door. Maria stuck her head in and called to Seitka, "Your bath is ready, Seitka. If you don't hurry, you will be late to your own wedding."

Seitka rolled over and found herself alone.

Maria grinned and told her, "He has been up for hours. Waiting impatiently, I may add."

Memories came flooding back of the night before, bringing a smile to Seitka's lips. Her eyes sparkled with merriment. Today was her wedding day. She nodded her head and brought the covers up over her breasts as the boys began filing in with steaming pails of water. After filling the tub and leaving, Maria added some of her precious rose water to the bath.

"For something special," she said with a smile.

Seitka sank into the hot water and moaned. Her muscles were stiffer than she expected. The run through the forest must have been harder on her than she thought. It had been quite a while since she had been allowed to really run. Maria helped her wash her long hair and laid out a beautiful dress.

"It was my wedding dress, but you may borrow it today," she explained. She helped Seitka dry and sat her in front of the dressing table while she brushed out her hair. Next, she arranged it, so it looked very sophisticated by adding flowers around the crown.

When she was finished dressing, Seitka looked into the mirror. "Oh my, Maria, you have made me look truly beautiful."

"Silly, you have always been beautiful. I just arranged your hair and lent you my dress."

Maria gave her a peck on the cheek. "We must hurry before they come up after us. The priest is already here. Chance is plying him with Aaron's whiskey," she said with a giggle.

Seitka stood at the top of the stairs, suddenly very nervous.

Daniel looked up at her, and the sight took his breath away. She was gorgeous, and she was all his. He had sent word to Colin about marrying his sister and the wolves guarding the clan in his absence, along with the journey to garner more allies and their honeymoon, of course. All was ready for the trip to the abbey in a week's time. After a small ceremony and a special dinner with just the family, they became man and wife.

Dylan ran to Seitka and said, "Now, you are my aunt. Mama said." He reached up with his chubby arms for a hug. Seitka gave the little boy a big hug and a kiss on the cheek before she said to Daniel, "I hope our child is as adorable as this one."

THE JOURNEY

*E*verything was packed and ready for the trip when an angry young man walked up to his parents and complained, "Da, Sarah said I cannot go." Tears began running down his chubby cheeks. "I want to go and play with Caitlin and Ava."

Chance bent down and lifted the little boy in his arms. "Dylan, we will be riding hard. Do you really think you are a good enough rider to keep up?"

"Yes, Da, I can ride good. Lightning will behave, I promise."

Chance had no doubt the little boy's horse would do exactly what Dylan wanted, but time was of the essence if they were to make it to the abbey before more trouble showed up. He trusted Mark to protect the clan. His soldiers were the most loyal and bravest he had ever seen. He knew his son would be safe at home, but he was not so sure about out in the open.

Maria took Dylan from his father to talk to her son. "Dylan, we cannot stop often or bring you back home if you get tired of riding. We are not taking the buggy, so you can't take a nap. Do you promise not to be a naughty boy or cry when you are tired?"

"Yes, Mama, I promise." He crossed his heart. "I am already

packed," he told them as he walked over to his father's horse. Daniel lifted him up, so he could open his father's saddlebags to reveal his favorite stuffy.

"Well, then, I will hurry and pack a few things for him, if you will see to Lightning being saddled." Maria laughed as she turned to run back into the keep to see to Dylan's things. When she returned, everyone was mounted up and ready to go, including Dylan. His horse was made for speed and endurance, but Chance had trained him for his little son. A couple of the guards were already on their way, scouting to make sure no problems were in front of them, and a couple more would be in the rear, seeing to behind the group. Chance started out with the women and Dylan in between him and Daniel, who was in the rear. The first day was a good day. They had put on quite a few miles. They had no problems, except for Dylan getting crabby from missing his nap. Chance put him on his horse and Daniel led Lightning. It wasn't long before Dylan was sound asleep in his father's arms. The rocking motion of the horse was just what the small boy needed. By late afternoon, he was ready to resume riding Lightning. They stopped along a stream and let the horses rest, eat and drink, late that evening. Daniel and Seitka went behind a tree, turning to cats, and went on the hunt, bringing back a couple of rabbits to cook. They had already eaten by the time they returned. Daniel made sure after he turned again that he had skinned and dressed the rabbits, so Dylan didn't see what they were. Maria and Dylan were playing with the squirrels and rabbits that had stopped nearby. Dylan held out a nut, and the squirrel gently took it from him with his front paws and quickly ate it. Finally, Maria told the boy to save some nuts for himself.

Later that night, Seitka and Daniel left the camp to romp and play in the forest. They were also looking for anything that could cause them trouble on their journey. Seitka loved running in the forest, hopping over felled trees, playing hide and seek with Daniel. She had hidden behind a large pine tree, the pine needles soft beneath her feet. Daniel found her and rolled her onto her back.

Standing over her, he allowed her to get up on all fours and he took her from behind. His teeth holding on to the skin on the back of her neck, he pounded into her while she purred. They returned late that night, refreshed from a swim and ready to sleep. Dylan slept between his parents.

The next day was a repeat of the first day. It was the third day that they encountered a problem.

While Daniel and Seitka went out on their nightly romp, they came upon a camp of horse thieves, sitting around the campfire, bragging about the latest batch of horses they had stolen. Daniel signaled for Seitka to stay back while he crept closer to hear what they were saying.

One of the men, who looked to be the leader of the other three, was eating and laughing about killing the farmer before they raped his wife and stole their horses.

Daniel heard a growling behind him. Seitka had disobeyed him and crept up behind him. When she heard about the rape, she became enraged, growling threateningly at the men in the camp. Daniel turned to her to shush her, but it was too late. The men had heard her. One of the men was coming around to see what the noise was about, and Daniel had no choice but to attack him. Going for the throat, he jumped from the ground with his powerful back legs. His weight brought the man down as Daniel tore out his throat. He turned to Seitka with blood on his mouth and teeth, growling at her angrily to get back, to run back to camp and protect herself. She stood there, defiant, turning to see the other three men coming with knives. They had heard the first man screaming, of course. Both cats stood, hackles up, teeth bared, and ready to fight, growling the only warning these men would have. Two of the men thought to take out the smaller cat while the biggest man took on Daniel. He looked at the huge cat with fear in his eyes, but Daniel left him no choice, fight or die. The big man came at Daniel with his knife raised. He sliced down, catching Daniel in the leg, but it was no use. Daniel was just too big. He made short work of the man before turning to help Seitka. In a very short time, all four were dead.

Daniel looked at the horses these men had stolen.

Seitka and Daniel both turned back then, to take care of the horses. "We need to lead these horses back to camp. We will drop them off at the next farm we come to. I am hoping that is who they belong to." As Daniel started to tie the horses together so they could lead them back to their clothes and camp, Seitka noticed that Daniel was limping. Blood was running down his leg from a knife wound. It looked deep and was still bleeding.

"Daniel, your leg; quickly tie this cloth I found in their camp around it until we get to the stream again and I can wash it and look at it."

"Seitka, I am too angry with you right now to talk to you. Go get our clothes and bring them back here while I go through their camp and see what else they may have that will help that poor woman who just lost her husband. Go now and do as I say, for once."

Seitka had never heard him so angry before. He had been angry, but never like this.

"Yes, sir, I will hurry back, but please, Daniel, clean the wound with that hot water on the fire and wrap this clean rag around it until I can look at it. For me, please, do it."

Seitka quickly turned back to cat, so she could run faster to their clothes and bring them back.

When she had walked maybe halfway, she met Daniel riding toward her with the string of ten horses behind him. He quickly dressed, and they divided up the horses and made it back to camp, waking up Chance.

After Chance helped him stake out the horses, Daniel told him what had happened, looking angrily at Seitka when he got to the part where he had told her to stay back and she had disobeyed him. He glared at her when he told Chance he had instructed her to run back to camp and she stayed to fight with him. All the while Seitka was stitching up the cut on his leg, he was finding her guilty of disobedience, and she knew what that meant. She was going to get another spanking.

Chance shook his head in disbelief as the story unfolded. Maria had woken up and sat in front of him. She looked sadly over to Seitka, knowing what was coming.

"We will take the horses to the nearest farm and hope they belong there. I also found some gold that will help the widow, now that her husband has been murdered. She should have enough to last her the rest of her life if she is careful. Those men had horded quite a stash."

Chance agreed, "We don't have much time to waste, but we must see the horses and gold get back to where they belong."

Daniel turned to Seitka. "I will hold off on your spanking until tomorrow. We will have to ride hard to find where the horses belong, and I don't want you to be in so much pain you cannot ride. Tomorrow night, when we go for our romp, your bottom is going to pay a mighty price."

Seitka nodded her acceptance of his judgment, her face blazing red with embarrassment as he pronounced judgment in front of the others.

Even Dylan was squirming. He bent to whisper in his mother's ear, "Is she going to get a spanking, Mama?" Maria put her finger to her lips to shush him as she nodded. Dylan's eyes got wide as he crawled into his mother's lap.

Seitka did not look forward to tomorrow night, but she knew she had earned it.

The next morning, Chance came up with a better plan. "Why don't you and one of the guards take the horses and see what you can find? Meet us at the river near the abbey or before. I will have one of the falcons circling over us, so you know where we are. That will allow us to continue to the abbey, and you can take what time you need to find the woman."

Daniel thought that was a very good idea, too. "That way, the girls and Dylan won't have such a hard ride. I agree."

As Daniel was getting ready to ride out with the horses and one of the guards, he turned to Seitka and said, "We will finish our discussion when I return. You have gained some time to come up with a good excuse. Mind you, it had better be very good."

"Yes, sir, I will think about it."

Daniel was off with the horses and the guard to find the woman who owned them. He knew she would need help with both the gold and family or someone to just hold her for a few minutes, after all she had been through.

DANIEL AND THE WIDOW

*D*aniel and Gabe, the guard, finally found a farmer's hut that looked like it could belong to someone who had horses. They stopped their weary horses again. They had spent the day searching. When they found a farm, one of them stayed back out of sight with the horses, and the other went to talk to the farm family. They had no luck until the day's end.

Finally, they found a farmer who pointed to the dell and said, "It sounds like Linda. She has a son." They had ridden hard and far, before they spotted the farm nestled near the river and the forest. Gabe stayed with the horses and Daniel rode to the front door. A middle-aged woman came out with a shotgun on her shoulder. Daniel smiled; she looked pretty, still, and fit, her eyes red from crying, it was obvious, but there was anger there, too.

He dismounted with his hands up. "Lady, I would just like a word with you. We have come across some bad men who told of killing a man. I wondered if you needed help?"

The woman instantly crumpled, lowering the rifle. Her eyes filled with tears as she fell to her knees, her hands over her face. Deep, soul-wrenching sobs tore through her small frame as a young lad of ten years or so ran to his mother and put his arms around her.

Daniel went to her before he let loose a whistle for Gabe to bring the horses.

The widow lifted her face to him, questioning his actions. The boy stared as Gabe rode in with the horses.

"We stumbled across the men who stole these. They are dead now, and we took all the gold I found on them. It is a considerable amount. I am sure it was stolen from others, too, but they will not need it any longer, so I will give it to you.

"My name is Linda, and this is Newly." She pointed to her son. "As you can see, this place is run down and we have no folks to help us. I don't know what to do."

Gabe spoke up, "We are going to the abbey. You and your son are welcome to come with us. Do you know who would have coin to buy these fine horses? If not, maybe some of the lairds will know."

"The McNaras would probably be willing, if you could take us there."

The four of them spent the day selling the horses and readying the widow and her son to go with them to meet up with Chance and the others on the trail to the abbey. The trail was too narrow for a wagon, so she had to take whatever they could carry on their horses. They kept an extra horse to carry a few additional things. Before they left, Linda and Newly went to the fresh grave to say their goodbyes.

Fresh tears rolled as Linda caught her breath and squared her shoulders. She had enough money to build a small home for herself and her son. She could buy a small piece of land near the abbey and maybe buy some new horses to breed. Her son would have something of his own when he grew a little more. She could go on for her son. She was thankful for all the help Daniel and Gabe had given her. There were still good people in the world, she discovered through all her sorrow.

As they neared the river, Daniel explained that they would follow it until they found the falcons and their friends. As they made camp, that night, Daniel noticed that Gabe kept a close eye on Linda. It made Daniel smile. It was much too early to think of romance. The woman just lost a beloved husband, but he also knew how lonely this land was and how there were fewer women than men. Women were to be cherished, as they were rare in many parts. Gabe helped Newly take care of the horses and hobble them, so they could eat and drink, while Daniel got the campfire ready. Linda had brought some sandwiches, fruit, and cheese, so the men did not have to leave to hunt. This was good, because they planned on only sleeping for a few hours. The moon was full, so they could continue traveling. Daniel wanted to get back to Seitka as soon as possible.

By the next morning, Gabe had pointed out the falcons. Daniel shook his head in wonder at what Maria and her son were capable of.

They met up just after noon, near the valley of the fey. At the bottom of the valley, fey stones were scattered, and it was considered a magical place. They rode around the stones and headed quickly for the forest beyond.

Daniel looked at Seitka, who had a worried look in her beautiful eyes. He hated to have to spank her. He was not angry any longer but more concerned. He worried that she would not obey him when it was important, and it would cost her her life. He knew he loved her and wondered if he could even live without her. He looked at Linda, so full of sorrow because of her loss. He did not want that for either of them. Then, too, there was the babe she carried. Colin said he had a vision, and the babe would bring them all together and they would all prosper. He knew she loved the babe already; she put her hand protectively over her belly whenever she talked of it. He knew he had to get through to her that he would be the one protecting her and making the rules in their family. He shook his head as he looked at her. He had no choice. The only way he knew to teach her what he needed her to know to keep their marriage strong and to protect her was to spank her hard. After supper that night, he stood and excused them both. He knew Chance and Maria knew what was going on, but he didn't want to embarrass Seitka any more than he already had. He held his hand out to her and helped her up.

"We are going to take a walk into the forest." He knew Maria and Chance would keep their secret, both about shapeshifting and the spanking.

When they had gotten a good way away, they both shifted. Seitka loved to run, and she took off first, but Daniel noticed the sparkle was not in her eyes this time, and it saddened him that he was the reason why. When they reached a stream, Seitka stopped and changed back. Her hands were on her hips. She was trying to put up a good front. She stomped her foot. "I do not want a spanking," she shouted at him.

"Seitka, I do not want to spank you. Tell me why I shouldn't. I asked you to think about a good reason. What have you decided?"

"I love you. I will protect you the same as you will me. I do not deserve to be spanked for acting the same as you would."

Daniel looked into her eyes, so full of fear and sadness. He sat on an old stump and patted his lap. "Come here, little one, and let us talk a minute."

She slowly walked toward him, her eyes never leaving his. She sat down on his lap, and his arms went protectively around her. She leaned her head back against his massive chest. How safe and protected she felt here.

Daniel's deep voice rumbled in her ear, "First off, little one, you agreed to obey me when we married. Do you remember your promise?"

Seitka nodded her head as he continued. "Secondly, I will protect you always. You are so small. When those two men ran towards you, the terror I felt in my heart almost brought me to my knees. How can I fight when I worry about you? When your safety is at stake, how can I concentrate on what I need to do?"

Seitka sat up straighter on his lap, her hands on her lap twisting in worry.

"Answer me, Seitka, how can I protect you if you disobey me?"

"But, Daniel, I cannot stand to think of you in danger, either. I must try and protect you, too. I love you and can't imagine what I would do without you."

"And yet you think a little thing like you can protect me by fighting off not one but two full grown angry men? Think about it, Seitka, all you did was put both of us in more danger because you did not obey me."

Seitka worried her fingers even more. She knew he was right. She had thought about it many times the last day. She stood and paced, trying to think of an excuse to get out of this spanking that seemed even more inevitable. Daniel also stood and walked to her, tipping up her chin, so she would look into his eyes.

Daniel laid out the most important piece of evidence. The piece that would trouble her the most.

"Did you not think to protect the babe, Seitka?" he asked quietly.

Seitka's eyes opened wide. She had only been thinking of protecting Daniel this whole time. She had forgotten about the baby she carried. It had happened too quickly; she was so frightened for Daniel. Tears filled her eyes at the thought she had put the babe at risk. Her hand went to her tummy protectively, while she held out her other hand to Daniel. He pulled her into his chest again.

"Being a mother is new to me. I only thought of you. It all happened so fast."

Daniel led her to the stump where he sat again. "I will not punish you if you do not agree you deserve it. I only punish you to guide you, to remind you not to ever do this again. I am big, you are small. I will protect you and our family. I do not enjoy spanking you and causing you pain. I would enjoy burying you much less.

Colin had a dream." He reached for her tummy and put his big hand on it, covering the babe. "He dreamt that this babe will bring both clans peace and prosperity. This is not just a babe for us to teach and love; he or she has a destiny. We must protect that at all costs."

Seitka nodded again, this time in acceptance. "Please spank me and teach me never to put our family at risk again. Teach me to obey you, maybe not in all things. We will discuss things like this before a punishment and I will tell you how I feel, and we will decide together if I deserve a spanking. Agreed?"

Daniel laughed. "No, little one, we will discuss these things, but I will decide if you deserve a spanking, and I will decide how and where and for how long. I am the man of our household. You have a say and will say your piece, but the final decision will be up to me. I love you and will never truly harm you. Do you trust me, Seitka?"

Seitka nodded. "Yes, husband, I love you and trust you."

"Come here, Seitka, and take your spanking. It will ease your guilt, and then it will be over. We will not talk about this incident again."

Seitka walked over to Daniel slowly, dragging her feet. She remembered how this hurt, but she remembered how much better she felt afterward, also."

She lay over his lap. He positioned her, so her bottom was high up on his lap and her tummy was over the side and would not get jostled. She held herself up with her arms, which meant she could not reach back.

He lifted his hand high and brought it down with a stinging slap that had her yelping. "Ow, Daniel, not so hard, that hurts so much."

Daniel chuckled. "It is going to hurt, Seitka, much worse. This is a lesson I am making sure you remember, so I never have to feel the terror I felt when I saw those two men coming at you again."

He continued spanking her hard, starting at the crown of her bottom and working his way down. His big hands covered both sides of her little bottom. Finally, when he heard her first sob, he decided he needed to bring it to an end. He finished with a flurry of hard, stinging hot spanks to her sit spots that had her howling. When he finished, he rubbed her hot, apple red bottom. She would not sit comfortably the next day in the saddle, but she would not be in unbearable pain, either. He pulled her up and held her until she stopped crying.

"I love you, Seitka, please never, ever do anything like that again. Now, that is the last we will say about it unless it happens again. In that case, you will get a strapping, and take my word, little one, you do not want that. Now, promise me, so we can be done and go back to the camp and get some sleep. Tomorrow will be brutal, but we should be at the abbey by tomorrow night."

"I promise, Daniel, I will never do that again. Let's change and play in the water before we go back."

Daniel shook his head. "No, little one, there will be no pleasure for you, tonight. That is part of the punishment. I know it will punish me, too, but it cannot be helped."

Seitka looked up in surprise before she saw the determination in his eyes. "Very well, let us go back to camp. I can enjoy a run, at any rate."

Daniel nodded, and they both took off through the forest. He laughed; he was sure, even in her cat form, he could see her red bottom wiggle through the trees. As they reached the camp, they both fell onto their blankets exhausted from all that had happened that day.

Chance and Maria rolled over in their blankets, both smiling, before sleep claimed them, also.

The group got up before dawn, the next morning. They let Dylan sleep while they packed up the blankets, and Linda and Maria made breakfast of some berries they had found and jerky. Daniel saddled the horses while Chance helped.

Chance was the first to speak. "How fast can we travel, Daniel?" Chance was asking about the condition of Seitka's bottom.

"Seitka will be all right. I did not punish her so hard that she could not ride hard today. She will be a bit tender, though, so a rest at noon would probably relieve her. We have to think of the babe she carries, too."

Chance nodded his head. "I agree; we will stop at the little lake. The women can bath in the lake while we hunt for food or set up camp. That will make her bottom feel better, and she will be able to handle the rest of the ride. We should be at the abbey around dusk if we just take a couple of hours at noon."

Daniel agreed, and the men finished their jobs, leading the horses back to camp. Maria handed a still sleeping Dylan to his father, and they were off again.

When they stopped at noon, while the men were hobbling the horses, the girls were gathering herbs and healing plants nearby. Linda was surprised by how much the girls knew of healing. Horses she knew, healing not so much. They laughed as they gathered their prizes. Fox Glove was abundant and was used for digitalis. Seitka found some Butcher's Broom, which was used for gall bladder problems and urinary tract problems. They also found moss to dress wounds and Yarrow to reduce bleeding and infections in wounds. They carefully put them in wet cloths and put them in the saddlebags that were left at the camp. Linda pulled some of the precious plants by the roots and carefully wrapped the roots in a wet cloth and put them in her saddlebags, too. Maria told her if she kept the roots wet and she was gentle, she could plant them at the abbey, and then when she was ready, she could replant them at her new home. Seitka found some St. John's wort and added it to her collection. She told Maria she would make a tea tonight for Linda. It would help with depression.

When the men returned, they told them they would take them to the lake to wash. Seitka was so happy to be able to soak her sore bottom in the cool water, she reached up and gave her husband a kiss.

Daniel gave her a sweet kiss back. "You have been very good, and I am proud of you, little one. You deserve a reward. Tonight, when we get our own room at the abbey, I will reward your good behavior." He wiggled his eyebrows, which brought a laugh from Seitka. The sound of her laughter was music to his ears. Daniel knew she'd had a hard few months, and her laughter made his heart sing.

Chance broke in to tell them he had sent a couple of guards out to hunt for their dinner and if Daniel was ready, the girls were all eager for their bath.

Both men sat on the shore trying not to look at the three women as they laughed and splashed in the water. An occasional shriek was heard as they played in the water, along with the two small boys.

Chance took this time to talk to Daniel about the other lairds and the abbey.

"Wolf is married to the king's goddaughter. Pup is six-years now, and their daughter, Caitlan, is the same age as Dylan, which is why he wanted to come and play with her. Rolland and Colleen have Danny and Ava. Danny is about Pup's age, and Ava is Dylan's age. I should not tell you all the secrets, but I trust you, of all people, with our secrets. Colleen has visions, like your Colin, only she has them at all times, not just in her sleep."

Daniel listened intently.

"Samuel married Kary, and they had a hard time having children, but they have a son now. He is very young, so I am not sure if Kary will be with us. Samuel, I am sure, will. Acelin married Hope, who is deaf, but she is an empath and a psychic. They lose a sense when they receive their gift. Hope's lost her hearing. They have a son named Arden who has shown great promise, but so far, he has not lost any sense that I know of, and a daughter whose name is Amy, and she is also Dylan's age. Erich is Hope's uncle and a powerful laird, also. He is a great commander as he is sly and full of ideas. Beware, because he is a great manipulator."

He paused to let his words sink in before going on. "Jamie is the son of Isaac. Isaac holds the history of all the Irish clans. He has a huge library with all of our heritages. Jamie married Kelly, and they have a son, Sean, about Dylan's age. Do you notice anything about most of their ages?"

Daniel laughed. "How did it happen they are all around the same ages?"

"We found out, after the great battle of the abbey, the women were all pregnant, or four of the five anyway. I will explain what happened at the battle of the abbey as we travel. I think it's time for us to call the girls. I smell smoke, so the guards must be cooking our dinner now."

They began their journey right after they finished their meal. Everyone was in a good mood and happy. Chance told the story of the battle of the abbey and about how the lairds became beholden to the great stag. Dylan knew the story by heart. The closer they got to the abbey, the more excited he became.

"Da, how much longer until I can see Caitlan and Ava and Amy? Da," he yelled louder when his father ignored him.

Chance turned to his son. "Son, I was talking to Daniel, and it is rude to interrupt someone. You must learn patience."

Maria smiled. It was hard for Chance to correct his son, but she also knew he would if he had to.

"But, Da, you aren't hearing me," he grumbled with a pout on his young face.

Chance rode up to his son and plucked him from his horse to put him in front of him. "What did you ask me, son?"

"I wanted to know how much farther. The falcons have begun circling, see. We must be getting closer."

Chance was stunned at his son's statement, but when he looked up, sure enough, the falcons had begun circling. He looked at his son in amazement, "I'll be…" he stopped and looked down at Dylan "…darned."

Maria and the other women laughed until they almost fell out of their saddles. Maria hoped Daniel would be a good father, just like Chance.

Dylan wiggled. "Da, I want to ride my own horse into the bailey of the abbey. The girls may be there watching."

Chance put him back onto his own pony again as everyone began laughing again. Chance shook his head. "Already worrying about the girls and what they think. Maria, you will need to keep a very close eye on *your* son in a few years."

Just as the moon was coming over the treetops and the dew had begun clinging to the grass, the group entered the bailey of the abbey. Father Dominic and Wolf waited for them at the door.

Wolf spoke first, "We are all here, Chance. We have a hot meal and a bed for you all." He glanced over at Linda. "I didn't know you were here, but we will find a bed for you two, also. We will talk in the morning."

Dylan got down off his horse in a leisurely fashion, very maturely for his age. "Where are the girls, sir?"

Wolf looked down at the young laird and grinned. "They are all in bed. You may see them in the morning. Very early, I am sure." He rolled his eyes.

Dominic spoke next, "We are the only ones up; it has been a long journey and a long day. Let us eat and find rest. Tomorrow will be soon enough."

THE ABBEY

*T*hat night, after they had found their room, had a full belly, and were ready to relax, Daniel called Seitka to him. He was sitting on the side of the bed, his long hair flowing down his back, naked. His cock was large and thick. It had been a few days since they had made love, and he was more than ready. Seitka finished undressing and walked over to her husband, sitting on his lap. He began rubbing her back gently, his voice low and sultry," Do you want to go for a small run?"

Seitka looked into his eyes, desire deepening the whiskey color to a darker almost black. Giggling, she agreed.

Daniel opened the shutters, both of them changing. They hopped out the window, roaming the back yard until they reached the forest. As usual, the forest called to them. They had very good vision in the dark. The smell of the forest floor was sweet pine and leaves. Small eyes looked at them from a vantage point high above in the trees; an owl called to them, rabbits and squirrels ran from them. They could see the wolves, but they had become used to their runs. The wolves that were not used to them, the ones that stayed to guard the abbey, watched carefully.

Seitka took off first, stretching her legs as she ran, around trees, and over rocks and fallen tree trunks. She felt free and happy. Daniel was right behind her. He was stronger and faster, but he did not outrun her. He stayed with her to protect her. They ran until they came to the edge of the forest. Just beyond was a lake of pure, clear water, the moon reflecting on it, along with the stars. The bank was soft and green with grass, dew sparkled, and a mist hung all around. On either side of the lake was blue heather as far as they could see. It was beautiful.

Seitka lay down in the grass playfully swatting at Daniel until he'd had enough. Seitka looked at him in his animal form. His coat was rough and thick, with stripes of black and grey, with small patches of brown and white. His stripes were so distinct. His cat was muscular and big.

Her muscles were well developed, but she was smaller. Daniel was a very big cat. She had the same tabby markings but lighter in color and smaller. Daniel went around the area and marked the trees, so the other animals would know this was their territory. He came back and rubbed his face gently against hers before licking her. They both changed. It was Seitka's decision to mate in either form. She lay naked in the grass as Daniel, too, changed.

"I want to feel your skin, this time," she stated in a low sexy voice that had his cock standing straight up. She could feel his hunger, and it matched hers. He began to kiss her neck below her ear, where she was extra sensitive. His mouth brushed hers softly, and then he took her mouth in a deep, hard kiss, bringing the tingle between her legs. His tongue began exploring down her neck to her breasts.

Seitka's breathing was coming in small pants as he continued to her nipple. He took first one and then the other, laving it, sucking it, pulling with his teeth, all the while playing with the other, twisting and pulling with his rough fingers, until her breasts ached with need. He was igniting a fire below. Coaxing her to spread her legs, he lay in between, lifting her limbs as he began a different feast. He found her little, swollen nub and began circling with his fingers first, and then he bent down and began sucking at the clit. His fingers found her treasure and entered her. First one finger and then two. She was hot and slick for him. Her scent was calling to him. They burned together, her heat almost too much to bear. It sent a wave of need through him until he couldn't hold back any longer. He rose over her, his weight supported by his arms as he looked into her eyes and slid his now massive cock into her liquid heat. Her sex clenched, dripping for him. Her inner muscles squeezed his cock until he had trouble moving. He stopped and waited a second until she relaxed enough to let him enter fully. He was not yet seated. When she had finally let him in fully, he impaled her to the hilt, bringing a keening wail. He took her mouth to cover the sound, to absorb her cries of passion. She fisted her hands in his hair, anchoring herself as she twisted and squirmed, trying to get closer and to let him in deeper. Her bottom lifted off the grass as her inner muscles tightened again around his cock, His hand slid lower to play with her clit while he pumped in and out of her scorching hot pussy. He could feel her getting closer as her pussy clenched around him, milking him. Her breathing was now ragged, her lips parted to let out moans of delight. He pumped faster and harder, knowing she was near, and so was he, to the ultimate goal. With a loud cry that he covered with his mouth, she came completely apart, crying out as she writhed beneath him. He followed close behind, sending hot splashes of his seed deep inside of her. He rolled off her, putting his hand over his eyes as he struggled to catch his breath.

Seitka was gulping air, still moaning. "Oh, my sweet God," she struggled to say as Daniel got up and lifted her, walking with her in his arms to the lake. The cold water was a shock, but it felt so good on their hot skin. He bent her back over his arm and washed her long hair, before he righted her and began cupping his hands and letting the cold water drizzle over her breasts. Her head snapped back, taking in the feeling of cold water on her slightly sore breasts. He carried her out and they both lay on the grass.

"This will become our place to come to when we need freedom or peace or each other," Daniel declared.

Seitka agreed as she laughed, "The cold water felt good. I am slightly sore below and on my breasts. The cold water helped. It was so worth every second. I never knew love could feel like this, Daniel, but I love you more every day."

Daniel pulled her close to him, kissing her forehead as he spoke. "I love you more than I ever imagined, little one. I knew I loved you when you were young, when you were growing up, but I love you like a woman now, and it is so much more. I will ask the doctors how long it will be safe for us to have rough sex. I may have to become gentler for a while. I will ask him about spankings, too."

A wide smile crossed Seitka's face. "You mean, you may not be able to spank me while I am pregnant? Oh, Daniel, that would be a shame," she smirked. He rolled her over and gave her a stinging slap on her bottom, "I have other less than pleasant ways to punish you, little one. Someday soon, I will show you how pleasant a good girl spanking can be. I think you will love it."

She shook her head in denial, but Daniel only smiled a knowing smile. They lay and looked at the moon shining on "their" lake, but soon, it was time to go home. They would need a little sleep before everyone else got up, and she was sure Wolf was right about the children being up early. She also didn't want to be a slug-a-bed on her first day at the abbey and have others think she was lazy. They changed and had a very nice run home before they jumped back in through the window. Falling into their bed, they both fell asleep as the wolves howled into the rest of the night, Daniel pulling Seitka into his arms.

The next morning was just as they feared. Children's voices could be heard in the hall, outside their door. Squealing and laughing greetings, the joyous sound of children that only they could make. Soon, came a woman's weary voice, "Come, children, let us go to breakfast before you wake your papas."

There was the sound of little footsteps and running, and then all was quiet. Daniel's low rumble of laughter in her ear brought her own laughter. "This is what we have to look forward to, little one."

Seitka snuggled back into his arms. "Yes, but right now, we can sleep." She was soon back to her sweet dreams.

Seitka awoke later to an empty bed. She turned to the window. The sun was up but not by far; it was still early. She gathered her clean clothes to dress. She wanted to make a good impression the first day, so the others would think well of her. Last night, as they entered their room, one of the nuns showed them their room and the wardrobe with a few clothes in it.

"Sister Mary is our seamstress, and she will make you some clothing that will fit better but, in the meantime, you are about the same size as Hope. Hope has offered some of her dresses for you to wear, and you, sir, are about the same size as Wolf. He also has offered you some of his clothing. I am sure Mary will have some of the other nuns busy making some things for you, shortly. She has just finished new stuffies for the children. If there is anything else you need, please feel free to find one of us. We have nuns working around the clock, and you should be able to find one soon enough. Breakfast is early, around five, and lunch is noon sharp. I am sure the others will let you know when sup is." With that, she left.

Seitka washed in the basin left near the fireplace. No fire was necessary this time of year yet, but soon. It was all cleaned and waiting for autumn's bite.

As Seitka opened their door, a small woman was just leaving her room. She turned and greeted Seitka.

"My name is Amanda; I am the wife of Wolf. Come, I will introduce you to the rest of us and we can have our breakfast. The nuns have taken the children to the nursery, where they may play after breakfast. Thank God for the nuns; they are very good people. You will like Father Dominic, also."

Amanda held out her arm and Seitka promptly took it, happy to have met a friend already. Over breakfast, everyone was introduced and an agenda was laid out for the day.

Wolf stood as he spoke, so everyone could hear him. "All of the men are going into a closed-door meeting. We will have a meeting after dinner with everyone, including Father Dominic," he pointed to the priest, "to let everyone know the plan. Father, could you please have a few nuns available to watch the children in the nursery?"

Just then, Isaac O'Conner came in with his wife, Alana. Isaac was the oldest laird. He and Alana had retired to a nearby home, leaving the clan to his son, Jamie, and his wife, Kelly, and their son, Sean.

"We will watch the children in the nursery, same as always. I also have a book on the shapeshifters. Seems like my da had encounters with them in his many travels. It may interest you two, also." He pointed to Daniel and Seitka. "Very interesting reading. Goes back four or five generations."

He handed the heavy book to Wolf, before they both sat down and began their breakfast.

Kelly and Jamie walked over to give Isaac and Alana a kiss before returning to their chairs.

Alana looked up. "Where are the children now?"

Jamie looked up with a smile on his face. "All of your grandchildren are in the nursery with the nuns at the moment, giving their parents a much-needed break as they were up at the crack of dawn."

Alana smiled as she said, "I will join them after breakfast."

"And I will join the men," Isaac stated.

Hope said, "Why don't Acelin and I give them each their yearly checkups while they are all here? After, we can take them outside for some fresh air."

Amanda and Colleen agreed, "Fresh air is good for them. That is a good idea."

After breakfast, the girls took their children to the infirmary. One by one, the mothers and their children entered while the rest waited. First was Amanda with Pup and Caitlan. Caitlan waved to her playmates as she entered. Hope sat her on the table and undressed her as Acelin checked Pup over behind the curtain. Pup was the oldest and the easiest to check over and left soon after, waiting in the hall for his mama and sister. Acelin checked the little girl's hairline for bumps, her neck, listened to her heart, and felt her pulse, before asking Amanda if she had any concerns. Amanda didn't, so Acelin gave both children a clean bill of health and sent for the next parent and children.

Next was Colleen, who brought in Danny and Ava. He repeated the procedure, only after he sent the kids out, he asked Colleen to stay and talk a moment.

"Have you noticed either one of the children having more or less telepathic or psychic episodes, and if so, are they stronger than the last time we talked?"

Colleen replied, "Danny hasn't any, as you know, but Ava is still having them the same as I did when I was young. I am teaching her how to handle them and to tell me immediately after she sees something. She usually has the vision when someone touches her. She has learned to keep it to herself until she finds me or I hear her crying out in her sleep. I am teaching her the same as my mam taught me."

Acelin nodded. Some of these children had special needs that he tried to keep on top of. "They are no worse than before?"

"No, the dreams don't happen often, usually only if someone touches her who has strong emotions, like hate or fear."

Acelin nodded and led her out, calling in the next couple, Jamie and her son, Sean.

He made short work of Sean, a big strapping boy of five. Next came Maria and Dylan. The boy was fit as a fiddle and thriving, very intelligent. Acelin let the child down and out to play with his playmates and Alana, but he kept Maria back, asking the same questions, "Have you noticed if his gift is getting stronger? He is very intelligent, Maria, maybe more than normal, have you noticed?"

Maria puffed up with pride. "Yes, he really keeps me on my toes. He scares the spit out of Chance sometimes. The other day, he called down the hawks when Daniel came and he thought he had hurt Seitka. We had to have a talk. He is not allowed to call any animals until he is older, the same as I was not. He was so amazed when the *Arsa* came to our keep. He got to ride on his back and he was in total awe, but when he called down the hawks, the *Gohlainn* knelt to Dylan. I think he will be special, but I don't like to say. Maybe Hope will know. I think he will have a purpose in life."

Acelin looked at her for a second. "I will ask Hope to come to you. Only if she wishes, you understand."

Maria replied, "Thank you, Acelin. It is much appreciated. I hate to ask her."

He smiled at Maria and explained, "Arden is showing signs of psychic ability, also, but I am hoping that he does not lose a sense, since he is a male. It has never happened in her family, but he has several times touched someone and told me later what they thought or felt. I am excited to see how he develops. I am also teaching him not to say anything until he talks to me first."

"Aren't we a bunch of misfits?" Maria commented with a laugh.

Acelin grinned and said, "Can you send your friend, Seitka, in? Hope would like to check her over while I am in the meeting with the men. I will speak to Hope about Dylan, first. She can let you know how she feels about seeing to his future. It doesn't always work, you realize that?" Maria nodded and left to find her friend to tell her she was wanted.

Seitka walked into the infirmary, when she was told to visit the doctor. She didn't like doctors most of the time, but Hope was there and Acelin was gone, which made undressing much easier.

Hope smiled at her new friend. "Do not be afraid. I just want to check the baby's size and location, maybe see if I can hear a heartbeat. I will also put my hand on your tummy. I can sometimes feel if the baby is happy and healthy or in pain."

Seitka looked at her in wonder. "You are a psychic, like my

brother. Chance told me a little about you all. Please tell me what you find. I would like to know my baby is fine."

Hope nodded her head and helped Seitka to lie down. "You don't have to undress; I can cover you and lift your dress, if you like."

"Whichever is best for you, my friend."

Hope gave Seitka a sheet and peeked under it when Seitka was comfortable. She put her head down and tried to listen to the heartbeat.

"I can hear the heartbeats of you and the babe. Both are strong and steady." She looked her friend right in the eye when she spoke, so Seitka knew she was telling her the truth. She laid her hands on Seitka's tummy, closing her eyes. A large smile lit up Hope's face as she set Seitka's clothing to rights.

Her eyes sparkled as she reassured her, "The babe is happy and safe, I need to tell you that this child is destined for great things. I see struggle and strife and danger, but he will win out and the world will be better for it."

Seitka hugged her new friend with glee. "Thank you for the marvelous gift, Hope, thank you so much. I cannot wait to tell Daniel. You have eased my mind so much." Tears were beginning to shine in her eyes as Hope hugged her back.

"Never fear, Seitka, but I have to tell you that he will be like Ava and your brother. I feel a psychic energy. He will have visions or dreams. Watch to see if he has them at birth. Some do. More likely, when he becomes a toddler, though. I feel it strong in him." Hope looked shocked that she had inadvertently given away the child's gender. "Oops, sorry, I normally don't let on the child's gender. I am so sorry if you didn't want to know."

Seitka laughed out loud. "I am happy to know. Thank you again. I will go find Daniel before they go into their meeting. I will meet you all outside in back."

Erich had just arrived as the men were going into the huge study.

Alana and the women were all headed out to the back yard to watch the children play.

The sun was shining. It was one of those beautiful days when it is not too hot or too cool. The breeze blew from the forest, making the air smell sweet. The women picked a tree nearby to sit under while the children played tag.

Suddenly, Ava fell to the ground, moaning for no reason. Colleen ran to her daughter to help her, when she heard Ava say, "Mama, a bad man comes. He will want to hurt us. He is near; we must run."

Colleen looked at Alana and the other mothers. "Get the children inside, *now!*"

Too late, a large man on an ill fed horse came galloping up to the children. He was dirty and obviously crazed. The women began to run to the children, but he reached down and snagged Caitlan. Everyone stopped in their tracks as he looked at them, holding the screaming child. Hope recognized the man as the one who had lost his son, some years back, because he had not wanted to spend the money on a doctor, even though they never charged anyone who couldn't pay.

Amanda began trying to stall for time by talking to him. She had sent Seitka to the abbey to get the men. Seitka had quickly changed to cat and run off to find Daniel.

Pup stood up and gave a whistle—loud and shrill. Two long ones, which meant they needed help from the wolves. While the man was looking at the boy, trying to figure out what the whistling was about, Dylan put his hands to the air, and the falcons came with talons out. Dylan spun his hands in a circle and they attacked the man, being careful of Caitlan. At the same time, the wolves came pouring out of the forest. The man dropped the child and turned to flee, but it was way too late. The wolves and falcons followed him into the forest as the men came running out of the abbey, only to see the tail end of the horse. His screams were clear and horrible. The women gathered the children and ran to the abbey and safety, not wanting the children to see what happened to the man. The men followed the trail of the man, so they could at least bury him so some of the women did not stumble onto his body.

Once the girls got the younger children inside, they took the time to make sure they were all right emotionally, first. Hope held Amy, talking to her soothingly, asking her if she felt all right. Next, she turned to Arden, who just shook his head. "I didn't see the danger, Mam." Hope pulled her son into her arms.

"Son, it doesn't happen that way. You know this. We have no control over our gift. Especially when we are young. Be thankful that Ava saw him." Arden shook his head and turned to leave before he turned back to his mother and threw himself into her arms, sobbing. Hope held him tightly until he had calmed down.

"This was not your fault, Arden, remember that. There are people who are bad or just not right in the head. We can only try to be ready. Together, you children are amazing. If you all work together, no one will be able to hurt any of you. That is the lesson today." She wiped the tears from Arden's eyes and gave him a small smile until he sadly smiled back and gave his mama a hug before leaving to seek out his father.

Colleen hugged her daughter until she squirmed to be let down. "I saw that bad man. I saw his face was all twisted and angry. I got a funny bad feeling in my tummy, and then I saw him in our forest, coming near us."

Colleen turned to all the children. " You all did well today. You protected Caitlin with your gifts. Hope is right. If you children stick together and protect one another, there is nothing that can harm you. What happened is not your fault, but the man needed to be taken care of. He was not right in his mind anymore. Now, let us forget this terrible incident and you children go to play. Be children for the rest of the day.

Wolf had taken Pup with him as soon as they entered the abbey. He wanted to reassure his son he had nothing to feel bad about. He had probably saved his sister's life. He, however, did not want Pup to ever whistle the death whistle to the wolves again, unless it was a life or death situation. Today, he did the right thing. He saved his sister's life, but calling the wolves and issuing the death whistle were two different things. Pup told his father he understood perfectly. When he saw the man put his hands on his sister, he had no choice. Wolf nodded his acceptance.

Chance and Maria took Dylan to their room and had a chat with him.

Dylan stood with his hands on his hips. "Mama and Papa, that man had Caitlin. I had no choice but to help her. I know not to use the falcons unless it is life or death."

Both Chance and Maria looked at one another in amazement.

Finally, Chance turned Maria. "Is that our three-year-old son talking?"

Maria stood and answered, "I believe so, husband. I will leave this chat up to you." She quickly left the room and ran to Acelin with the news.

After all was calm again, the men went back to their meeting, finally coming out at suppertime. Each of them took his own wife to their room and had a private conversation about what they had decided.

Sitting Seitka on his lap as he sat on the huge chair next to the fireplace, Daniel said, "We all must agree to the terms of the agreement. What Wolf proposed is an alliance with these clans. Seitka, I cannot tell you how beneficial this would be for your brother's clan. Wolf's proposal is that if you have a daughter, she will study with Acelin and Hope every summer after her tenth year. That would actually be when she is five. As you know, we age two years for every one until the fifth year. If you have a son, he will also come at the same age but to train with Wolf, Rolland, Jamie, and Chance, alternating clans but still training during the summers every year. It would keep the child safe and also give us a powerful ally. In return, I will train Pup, Danny, Arden, Sean, and Dylan—a different child every year. Wolf will send some of the falcons and carrier pigeons home with us, allowing us to communicate in a faster and more efficient way. You will train with Maria and learn how to get them to do what you need. We will stay here through the winter and spring to get to know one another, and it will be safer for you. I will send word to your brother to expect us home as soon as you recover sufficiently from having the child. Do you agree with these things, Seitka? I will not give my oath without your word."

"I do, husband. I feel a kinship with these women and a closeness to them, already. I would like to stay here until after the baby comes. Maybe, if they will have me, a short time longer."

Daniel rose from his chair. "It is settled then. We await the verdict from the others."

THAT SPRING, Seitka gave birth to a baby boy, just as she knew she would. He was healthy, with dark brown eyes and a thick head of hair the color of the tabbies, with the exception of a thick black stripe beginning at his bangs to the back of his head. He was a happy baby and Seitka loved him dearly. Daniel fell in love with the child before he was born. He was of Seitka. How could he not? The agreement had met with cheers from all the clans, and Seitka was given an amulet from the king to protect her, the same as the other girls. She worked hard, learning healing from both Hope and Acelin, as well as the other healers. She fell in love with them all, and they fell in love with her. Daniel stood guard duty with Wolf and the other lairds, to get to know each other's ways. Daniel taught them what he could do in either form, and he learned from them. He also learned that he was under the king's protection, as well as the rest of his clan. The king would expect Colin to come and pledge his allegiance to the crown after Daniel returned home.

The first five years flew by as was the way with tabbies. In the first five years, a tabby aged ten. They learned to change and to have control, and they grew at a rapid rate. Daniel took great care to protect Brian and Seitka. They were guarded at all times. The trouble that had been ever present with the black cats continued. Daniel knew Cearul would like nothing better than to get his hands on his wife and son. Soon, it was time for Brian to go to the abbey. Wolf would pick him up first, while Daniel took Pup. Seitka missed Brian and worried so much that, for the next few years, she stayed at the abbey so she could be near him, and in no time at all, fifteen years had passed.

BRIAN, FIFTEEN YEARS LATER

*B*rian came galloping up to the keep. Jumping off his horse, he ran inside. His twenty-year-old eyes sparkled with excitement as he ran up to his uncle, Colin. Out of breath, he took a minute to catch it before he began, "The lairds and their families have left. They are on their way."

Colin smiled at his nephew's excitement. This journey with the lairds had been very rewarding. Down through the years, Daniel and Colin helped train Danny, Pup and Arden, and the last one was Dylan. In return, Brian and a couple of the other older boys had traveled to the abbey and were trained by Wolf, Rolland and Jamie. He knew how much Brian loved to visit the abbey during the summers, able to feel free to be himself. He had become close friends with Pup, Danny and Arden through the years.

Arden and Brian had the same gifts as Colin, Arden's being the strongest. He could touch someone and know what they were feeling, just like his mother. He also had visions, and he would be a great healer someday. When Arden was sent to them, Colin took care to help the boys and to talk to them both about their gifts. The four boys had formed a bond that would last a lifetime. Dylan followed them everywhere, and being only a few years younger, he fit right in with the group.

A smile crossed Colin's face when he thought of Ava. Although Amy, Ava and Sean were the same age, Colin had caught Ava looking lovingly at Brian more than once. He was sure she had feelings for Brian. Brian hadn't caught on yet, but Colin had certainly noticed. When Colin visited the abbey, he saw how happy Brian was. He seemed carefree. He also noticed how Ava and Amy followed the boys to their fishing hole, on hikes, or even when the boys just wanted to go for a ride. Soon after, Ava and Amy showed up, seemingly by accident, leaving Dylan, Sean and Caitlan to find their own amusement. Danny had scolded her more than one time for following them to the swimming hole, where from time to time the boys shimmied out of their clothes and went for a cool swim. The beautiful sprites were more tomboys than ladies, but the girls' beautiful eyes and long dark hair wouldn't go overlooked for long.

Colin smiled to himself as he shook his head. Pup and Brian were in for a rude awakening one day. Colin knew when Brian was at the abbey, he was free to be like any other boy with gifts. At home, his own people looked at him differently. Mainly, because he was half black cat and half tabby, or because his real father was Cearul and many feared that one for his cruelty to his own clan. Some of his clan were mean and called Brian names in the years he was growing up. People from his own clan looked at him with disdain because he was different. Many remembered when his mother was raped by Cearul. Some waited for his father's blood to show itself. Many watched to see if he would grow to be cruel or selfish. It made Colin sad, but he knew it had shaped the boy into the man that he was. Brian had no patience for bigotry of any kind. He became stronger because of the harshness of his childhood. Colin also knew that Brian was very smart. Brian talked to Colin of his dreams often. Colin was surprised at how detailed his dreams were, at times.

Brian had trained hard. Wolf, Rolland and Jamie did not go easy on him. They knew, in order to fulfill the prophecy, he would need to use his wits and his muscles. They taught him all they knew. Brian worked hard, often coming home bone tired and sore, barely able to eat.

Amanda or Colleen or Kelly would rub some concoction over his muscles after a hot bath and he would feel a little better. He was always ready for bed early and was up at dawn. He didn't stop until supper. Not because the men pushed him, but because he pushed himself. The lairds and their men all respected him for putting in the effort and working the same as they did. He was always there to help and do what was needed, either for the clan or for someone less able than himself. He made sure the elderly had enough wood for the winter, or he delivered medicines for the girls. He made repairs to the homes of the handicapped or elderly, always making sure he didn't hurt their pride. He took whatever money they offered and gave it to the girls to deliver to the abbey when next they went. If no money was offered, he took payment in trade. One old woman made him gloves from deerskins, another made him sweet mead, which he gave the girls, or he took nothing but a hug if that was all that was offered. He brought sweets for the little ones or stuffies the nuns made for the clan children, always with a smile on his handsome face and a friendly word.

Colin smiled again; that boy was a force to be reckoned with. He had grown big like Colin, himself, and his stepfather and the lairds. He was strong from all his hard work. His hair was longer than most wore it, but he liked it that way. It flowed around his shoulders, the colors of the tabbies, but with a two-inch black strip down the middle. He wore it like a badge of honor. A sign of strength. His shoulders, like that of his friends, were broad and muscled. His legs were also like the other boys, strong. The six boys were a sight to behold. They were all as close as brothers. They each had their own talent that made them almost invincible when they worked together. Pup called the wolves, and Danny was brilliant at strategy. Arden was a strong psychic and seer; Sean had a photographic memory, and Dylan could make the animals do damn near anything. They would soon be all in one place. All the lairds and their families were coming to the tabby keep. They would be guests of Colin and Daniel. The king had agreed to one more trip before he stopped traveling. He was getting up in age, and he liked to stay at home. The king's nephew, Jeremy, would take over for him. The royal had been grooming him to become king since he was a lad, a smart but kind man who would follow the wishes of the king and continue building bridges between Ireland and England. He would be a strong leader. The king was coming to knight the boys and to get allegiance from all in the tabby clan— allegiance to the crown. In exchange, His Majesty was sending pure blooded milk cows for the farmers of the clan to breed and distribute so that no one went without milk. He was also giving them beef cattle of the purest blood to be bred and distributed to other farmers. Someday, when the clan had all they needed, they could sell the calves, along with seeds for corn, hay, barley and oats. They would also make whiskey. Seitka already wore the amulet around her neck that proclaimed a harsh and painful punishment from the king, himself, if anyone harmed her. She had taught the healing of animals to the lairds' wives, and they had taught her the art of healing humans.

Colin had never married, preferring to be alone with his thoughts and his clan. He was a genius but was destined to die alone. He had foreseen it in one of his dreams and had come to terms with his fate. Ciara continued to run the keep, while Colin saw to the clan alongside of Daniel.

Seitka worked with Ciara getting all the rooms ready for their royal guests and all the lairds. It was the first time they were all coming to her home and she wanted everything to be perfect. She was as excited as Brian was. All the bedding was fresh and clean. The tapestries heralding their history were all cleaned and back on the walls. The men went out hunting for the large amount of food that would be needed. Wolf was bringing barrels of Aaron's famous whiskey. The infirmary needed to be restocked, in case of accidents, and vegetables were to be plucked from the gardens. All the workers were busy doing everything from cleaning the barns and stalls to building two large barracks to house the extra guards and a small barracks for the six boys. Extra cooks were hired as well as maids to help keep the rooms tidy and clean. The fireplaces were all cleaned and stocked. It was the very end of summer and the nights were growing cooler.

The guards were on alert. Cearul was causing mischief again. Teddy had convinced a few of the black cats to join Colin's clan, but many were still afraid, even after all the years of abuse. Some of Cearul's guards were just plain mean and they enjoyed hurting others. He paid his loyal guards much money. The rest of the clan was hungry or abused, most of the time, living in fear of their laird and his friends.

The lairds and their families would arrive a week before the king, preferring to split up and not make such a large target. Each clan brought a few guards of their own and, of course, the wolves, falcons, eagles and other animals that followed them everywhere. The king had his own large number of guards.

The logistics would be challenging, but Colin had it all under control. The king would stay at the keep, as would the lairds. The boys would stay at a barracks erected just for them. The guards would house in another two barracks near the boys.

As Brian chatted happily with his uncle, there was a commotion outside. Suddenly, the door burst open and three angry farmers stormed in, stomping up to Colin, pointing fingers angrily at Brian.

"Your nephew has been giving Cearul information about our whereabouts, allowing the black cats to kill our cattle. We have spies on Teddy and the other black cats in the area. We know it is not them. That only leaves Brian."

The biggest man shouted, "When my family and I went to church yesterday, for the first time in a while, the black cats came and stole one of my cows."

"I have had cattle stolen, also," stated one of the other men.

"And so have I," the third added.

"You have to do something about this, Laird. We demand it."

Colin looked at the farmers in confusion. "Are you accusing my nephew of stealing your cows? He has only been home for a month. We have no need of your cattle."

"We have been watching the other black cats, Laird, and they have not done anything wrong. We keep an eye on them. But Brian is Cearul's son. He has bad blood."

Colin looked at each man in wonder. How had his clan become bigoted like this? His anger grew as he looked at the farmers. He had been good to them all, and this is the way they thanked him? He stood tall and shook his finger at them, his anger evident. His eyes snapped with emotion as he poked the biggest man's chest. It was obvious he was the leader of the group.

"You men know better than this. I want you to stop watching over Teddy and his family. He has been a valuable member of our clan. I want you to stop accusing Brian of misdeeds because of his heritage. He also is a valuable member of this clan. I will not stand for your hatred in this clan. If you cannot behave, I will banish you."

The men angrily left, grumbling and shaking their heads about lack of justice.

Colin turned to Brian. He saw the hurt in his eyes, the sadness and loneliness of not belonging. It tore at Colin's heart.

Brian raised himself to his considerable height before he said to his uncle, "I have had a dream, Uncle. Things will get worse before they get better. I will suffer before things improve. I think I should leave when the lairds leave. I am not sure I want to suffer for the likes of those men."

Colin looked at Brian sadly and replied, "Brian, I have had dreams, also. I know you will feel pain and suffering before it gets better, but it is your destiny. You cannot avoid your fate. You will bring us all together again. We will still be different clans, but we will work together and prosper together. If you leave, many women and children will suffer. Is that what you want? Those children did not pick whose clan they were born into. The women and children of Cearul's clan have suffered for years waiting for you to grow up and save them."

"I will think on it, Uncle, but I won't promise anything. In the meantime, I am happy my friends are coming. Mama and Daniel are at the barracks getting them ready and I think I will go help them. Tomorrow, I will go fishing and, hopefully, catch enough for a meal when everyone arrives. The other five boys can catch a bunch of fish, too. We are all good fisherman." He stopped to think a minute before he continued. "I suppose Ava will insist on coming along. She is such a little pest."

Colin laughed out loud. "I am sure you are right."

Slapping Brian on the back, he called for one of the guards, " Gordon, take a few men out to the farms and see if you can find their missing cattle please."

"Of course, Laird, right away."

Brian was satisfied that something was being done to clear his good name. He left for the barracks whistling an old Irish tune as he walked. He still didn't know if he would stay when his friends left for the winter. The clan did not want him. Why should he stay? He would talk to Daniel and his mam.

Brian was up at the crack of dawn, with his fishing pole, and headed for his favorite pond. The air was clear and clean, and the mist was still close to the ground when he left. He took a minute to enjoy the sight of the clan gathering vegetables and tending their animals. They always rose early and were constantly working on one project or another. Some of the men were finishing the barracks, while some moved beds into the separate rooms. Many of the women were putting clean sheets and blankets on ropes strung between trees to dry. One woman was hanging curtains in the barracks. Brian smiled at the activities. He was proud of most of the clan. They were hard working, kind, and often gave to the needy. Colin had helped them all prosper from their hard work.

CHAR CAULEY

The clan had the best leather and wood workers for miles around. The blacksmith was sought after by many from towns far away.

He waved to many as he passed, and they happily waved back. Once he got further from town, he felt nervous for some reason. Something wasn't right. He had the feeling he was being followed. He heard a twig snap behind him. He decided to circle back and see what was behind him. As he got closer to his fishing hole, he doubled back, leaving his pole at the side of the pond. He changed and quickly climbed the trees, staying high so no one could see him. He looked down at six of the farmers' sons. Sons of the men who had come complaining to the laird the day before. They were looking for him, being very sneaky. A couple had changed and were high in the trees. Brian hid in the leaves of a big tree, observing. As they came to the pond and found his fishing pole, they looked around in confusion. The biggest one called the others down from their perches.

Brian jumped from the branches to the ground behind them, staying in cat form. His fur rose on the back of his neck and his growl came from deep inside. His cat was very big and muscled. The six boys backed up, taking the situation in for a moment, whispering to one another before they all decided to charge him.

Brian had learned the ways of the cat and fighting from Daniel. He was fast and strong. He rolled the first cat and attacked the second, swiping the third and sending him sprawling. He was outnumbered six to one. It was a hard fought battle that Brian was destined to lose. They eventually got him to the ground, beating him mercilessly. They were biting and scratching him, gouging long and deep scratches with sharp nails, taking chunks of skin and flesh and fur, before they left him to die, torn and bleeding. Luckily for Brian, two of the guards happened upon him while looking for lost cattle. Gordon gently handed him up to the other, who galloped as fast as he could to the keep. Gordon galloped to the barracks to let Seitka know what had happened.

Daniel soon took Seitka to her son. He was lying on a bed in

114

very bad condition. He woke up long enough to cry out in pain, but he was able to give Colin the names of the farmers' sons. Seitka quickly gave her son some tea from willow bark and made poultices from comfrey roots to help heal his wounds. He stayed in cat form to heal faster and because he was of Colin and Seitka's blood, which came from the first wildcats. It was a purer form, which healed even faster.

A very angry Daniel and a few guards were sent to bring the boys to the keep and the laird's justice.

Meanwhile, a few of the guards had come back with one cow.

"We found it by a large marsh of quicksand. There are other cow tracks leading to the sand. This explains why the cows ended up missing. It was in a common pasture used by all the farmers. If the farmers would have gone looking for the cows, instead of watching Teddy or assuming they knew Brian did this, they would have found it themselves. They never even bothered to look."

Colin was livid as Seitka worked to save her son. She worked tirelessly all through the day.

It was late evening before Daniel and the guards brought in the boys and their fathers. Colin stood from his desk in the study, wearily wiping his face with his hand as he stood.

He looked the men in the eye as he asked each father, "Did you send your sons to beat Brian? Answer me true, or your sons will pay the price for your foolishness."

The boys' fathers looked down at their feet before the first one answered, "Your nephew is killing our cattle for *his* clan." The man never saw Colin's fist as it connected with his mouth. He went down in a pile of human misery. The other men helped him up.

Colin first took the men and their sons to Brian's room to see what they had done before he took them to the common room. Daniel and the guards were waiting to tell the farmers what had really happened.

"You men never even looked for your cattle. My guards found the evidence easy enough. You were too busy watching Teddy and his innocent family and accusing Brian. I have your cow, Rayden. We found her before she could get to the quicksand."

Rayden shook his head in disbelief. "That can't be, Laird. My cattle were not the only cattle to go missing, and it always happened when we were gone."

"They went missing when they were in the common pasture you all use. I suggest you were too lazy to keep an eye on them."

The farmers knew this to be true. They had become lazy the last few years. They had prospered and decided not to work so hard. Peter and Randy shook their heads as they all began to panic. What had they done? They had sent their sons to beat an innocent boy and not just any boy—the laird's nephew. They knew the punishment would be severe.

Colin looked at Daniel and said, "Put them in the dungeon for tonight. Tomorrow, call a clan meeting for noon. Make sure everyone is present to hear me pass sentence. I don't want this to ever happen again. Send some men to look after these men's cows and families. You may as well bring their families, also, as this will affect them."

Colin slammed his fist on the desk hard enough to knock off his glass. He looked in rage at the men and their sons. "You had better hope I calm down by morning, or you will all wish you were never born by noon."

All of the men were shaking by the time Daniel led them through the door and down into the cold, dank dungeon. Slamming the door, he stalked upstairs into the main house, giving the guards orders to go home and get some sleep. "Before the sun comes up, we ride with the news of a trial at the keep for these men and boys." He stopped for emphasis. "Let us all pray Brian makes it through the night, or we will see nine men hanging from the trees tomorrow, for sure." The guards all nodded in understanding as they left the keep.

Daniel went back to Brian's room to find a very tired Seitka. She had worked tirelessly to save her son, and now it was up to

God. She didn't want to leave, but Daniel insisted on leaving Ciara to look after Brian. He took her to their room in the keep and held her until she fell asleep. It was only a few hours later that he felt her leave the bed. He knew it would do no good to try to stop her.

"Seitka, take heart. Your blood runs in his veins. You have the blood of royalty from our beginnings. He will live."

He heard her sniff in sorrow before she answered in the dark, "He only has half of my blood, Daniel. My price for my disobedience all those years ago comes back to haunt me, yet again."

"If you had my blood, it would be stronger but not as pure as yours, my love. Don't keep blaming yourself. He is young and strong."

Without an answer, Seitka left to check on her son. When she entered the room, Brian opened his eyes. He was in pain but healing. He smiled at his mother to ease her worry.

"Fear not, Mama. I will survive and be ready for a hug soon enough. Go back to bed and come to see me after you have rested."

Seitka walked over to Brian and put her hand on his forehead. "Do you need any more willow bark tea, my son? Are you in pain?"

"Ciara has just given me some. I am soon to sleep, so please do the same. I will talk to you in the morning."

Seitka agreed, and kissing her son on his forehead, she turned to go. Before she turned, she said, "I love you, Brian. I am sorry this had to happen."

"Go to bed, Mama. I will be fine. I promise you."

After she closed the door, he turned, moaning, into the pillow, so she would not hear.

The next afternoon, with all the clan gathered, Colin had the men dragged out of the dungeon in chains to sit on the ground in front of the huge table. He explained what had happened to the clan, looking at the men of the clan to make sure they all understood the crime before he passed judgment. Banishment was the ruling. The women wailed; they would starve and their children with them. Just as Colin was about to lift the heavy gavel to signify it was done, Brian came hobbling out of his room.

"Wait, Uncle." He hobbled over to the table set up for the trial. Daniel stood at one end, and Colin sat in the middle.

"Please do not punish the women and children for these men. Please spare them this fate." He grabbed his side as he walked in obvious pain. He turned to the astonished men. "You deserve to be punished, all of you, for your hatred and bigotry, but your families do not."

He again pleaded with Colin for the innocent, "Let the men do hard labor for some time. All of them can do their farming for their families, and then they need to fill in the quicksand hole with dirt and rocks, so no more cattle fall into it. Put some guards on them to keep them working until time for bed. Make sure the job is done in a timely manner. After that, have them help the poor get ready for winter. Make them work until they are ready to drop before you return them to the dungeon each night."

Colin thought for a minute while the clan held their breath. Every man was amazed at the compassion this man had for these men after what they had done to him. Colin looked at Brian before shaking his head in his own amazement.

"Let it be as Brian says, with one provision. They will not return to their families to live until I am satisfied all the work is done and I am happy with them again. If I hear one complaint from any of their wives because their work at home is not done, I will double the sentence." The gavel fell. It was done.

Seitka helped Brian back to his room as the clan looked on. They had gained much respect for Brian that day. Daniel was proud of him and let him know, before he took the men back to the dungeon until a work force could take care of them and what needed to be done.

BRIAN'S LOVE

*B*y the time Brian came with news of the falcons being sighted, he was fully healed. He was so excited to see his friends again and, if he was truthful with himself, his little Ava. He had found he missed her mischievous smile, the sparkle in her eyes, her beautiful violet eyes and the way her bottom swayed when she walked. He even missed her naughtiness. She was a handful at times, but Brian wouldn't have it any other way. Thoughts of taking her in hand after being naughty had him hard as a tree.

The boys greeted each other like long lost brothers. Brian showed them the barracks they were to stay in, while Daniel and Colin greeted the lairds. Seitka and Ciara proudly showed the women their rooms, and the extra help they had hired carried up the trunks. The visitors would stay for one month as the men had much to discuss. The clan would meet them the next day. There would be a celebration for the clan and the lairds. The celebration for the king would be huge with a feast for everyone, the following week. Before the feast, the knighting and swearing of allegiance to the crown would take place. With much effort and working together, everything was finally in order.

The men all held meetings in the den while the women laughed and talked and visited the infirmary. Seitka made sure the cooks and maids all did as instructed. She had taken to being the lady of the house long ago, since Colin never married. She still had plenty of time to visit with the women and the girls, though. Ava and Amy had been forbidden to visit the barracks, but Ava watched and as soon as she saw one of the boys come out, she was right there following them to the pond or on their rides.

The following day was a very busy one. All of the tables were put in the courtyard for the meal. The men had hunted and killed wild boar, duckling, pheasants and deer. The pits of wood were all lit and ready for the meat to be put on spits. A few of the guards took turns turning the meat, while the women prepared the vegetables and desserts. The tables were full of every kind of food imaginable. One of the barrels of whiskey that Wolf had brought was tapped, and mead was poured.

That night, they held a dance to entertain the clan, the lairds and their families. The bagpipes, mandolins and fiddles were all brought in. The musicians stood on a short stage made of wood and a space had been cleared in the courtyard for dancing. The night had a slight bite to it, but no one noticed after the dancing began. The sky was clear, and the stars were out in full force. Blankets were scattered behind the area cleared for dancing. Everyone was having a merry time. When the step dance began, Brian and Pup got up to begin the intricate dance. It consisted of high kicks and complex footwork and took skill and stamina. Often, the one left standing was the winner. Everyone stood back and watched the two boys as they kicked and twirled. This night, there was no competition, just fun and good times. The villagers clapped as they watched them. The bagpipes played on and on, waiting for the two boys to tire. Soon, to their surprise, Ava and Amy jumped in and began to dance, also, mimicking the boy's moves. Amy paired with Pup, and Ava, of course, paired with Brian.

Brian was mesmerized by the sparkle in Ava's eyes. The joy on her lovely face as she twirled and lifted her feet to the moves intrigued him. Her laughter, along with Amy's, could be heard through the crowd. Brian danced with Ava until they had to seek refuge in the nearest chair, both of them laughing and trying to catch their breaths. Brian had his arm around her waist as she sat on his lap, and his hand began to pat her bottom in time to the music. As their breathing calmed, Brian realized just how breathtaking his little Ava was. Her little bottom fit perfectly on his lap. His cock jerked at the thought as his arm tightened around her waist. He had an urge to kiss her. Looking into her eyes, his lips began to lower. He wanted just a sip of Heaven. Their eyes locked.

Suddenly, Rolland came up to his daughter and took her hand, pulling her off Brian's lap, breaking the mood as he gave Brian an angry glare. Brian felt suddenly empty, missing the feel of her. He shook his head, smiling sheepishly up to Rolland.

"Sorry, Laird, your daughter's beauty has mystified me. She truly is a treasure. May I have your permission to court her while you are here?"

Rolland looked at the young man he had trained and had great respect for as did all the other lairds. The lad was a shifter, and he didn't know what to think about his daughter marrying a shifter. He shook his head. It didn't matter in the end. All that mattered was their love for one another. He had known for a while, along with his Colleen, that Ava was head over heels for Brian.

"I will talk to your stepfather, tomorrow, about this and let you know after our discussion."

Brian had to be satisfied with that, for now. "Yes, sir," he replied.

"In the meantime, no kissing or touching. Understand? She *is* my daughter."

Brian felt his manhood grow as he watched the lass walk away with a sway to her lovely hips. When he looked over at his friend, he saw Pup having the same talk with Acelin. Maybe they could have a double wedding. Brian shook his handsome head. What had brought up that thought? He had no plans to marry yesterday and yet, today, he was thinking of it. A smile crept across his face as he thought of marrying Ava. He thought of their wedding night—slowly undressing her like a gift. He wanted her more than he had ever wanted any other woman. He'd had a few in his young years, but none had lit a fire in his loins like Ava. She had been his friend and confidant for many years, always ready to listen and give sound advice. She was a handful at times, but she had a fire in her spirit he couldn't resist. Keeping her in line in the way of the men of his family stirred his cock again. She had such a cute bottom when she walked, and it swayed, too. It was a sweet torture, and he had a funny feeling she knew it, little minx that she was. He slowly walked to where Pup was standing. Both young men had goofy smiles on their faces and stars in their eyes. Pup took Brian's arm and led him to the great room where the men had a barrel of whiskey.

"Let us have a drink to our good fortune this night, brother," Pup said with a low chuckle.

"I take it you got the speech about talking to our das, also."

"Yep, Rolland will talk to Daniel, I assume, and Acelin will talk to my da." Both burst out laughing as they both parroted, "Do you want to get married together, the four of us?"

"When do you think they will allow it? I hope it's not too long, I can barely keep my hands to myself," Brian thought out loud.

"I hope not, either. I get hard just thinking about it."

"Let's go and tell our mothers the good news. They will tell our das, and then they will be prepared tomorrow, when Acelin and Rolland approach them."

"I saw them watching. I think they already know."

The boys were happily telling their mothers the news when they heard Amy scream.

The men were quickly leaving the study at the piercing sound. Pup jumped into action, with Brian following close behind and Danny, Arden and Sean in hot pursuit.

Amy was slapping at a young man, screaming at him to leave her alone. Terror was evident on her face and in her eyes as she pushed back away from him. Tears were in her eyes as she continued to scream and slap at the man. The young man was trying to turn to run when Pup caught him by the scruff of the neck.

"What the hell is the meaning of this?"

Acelin ran to her and gently pulled her into his arms, but before he could lead her away from danger, she broke away and ran to Brian, pointing to the man and saying, "This man is evil. He plans to harm you. He snuck into our dance, but he doesn't belong here. He comes from somewhere else to spy, so he can find your weakness and hurt you. There is another where he lives who wants what you have."

Brian's eyes became wide with shock before they turned to anger. "Cearul sent you here to spy on us. What does he want? Why can't he leave us alone?"

The man smiled an evil smile that transformed his looks into something ugly before he answered with, "He wants your clan. He wants you, and he will wage war to get it. Be advised that he is tired of waiting for you to come to him. He will bring the fight to you."

Brian's fist slammed into the man's face, knocking him back and onto the floor. "I am a man full grown now. You tell your laird that I am not afraid of him any longer. If he wants to fight, he can find me anytime in the open. One on one. If he is not too big of a coward, that is."

Daniel stood by Brian, saying, "This clan takes care of its own. You tell him, if he wants Brian, he will have to take us all on."

Daniel then took the man, lifting him off the floor by the collar and handing him to the guards. "See him out of our territory. I don't care how gentle you are with him on the way."

Pup walked to Acelin, Hope, and Amy. "Are you all right, my love?"

Amy looked into Pup's eyes and replied, "Thank you for coming to my rescue, Pup."

"Amy, don't you know I love you? I would protect you anywhere, from anyone."

Amy smiled and got up to give Pup a hug before she turned to her mother and asked to leave.

Acelin said to Pup and Brian, "I am proud of both of you for being there for Amy. I would be proud to have either of you for a son-in-law. Pup, I will talk to your da, tomorrow."

Rolland slapped Brian on the back as he left with the same words.

After the girls left with their families, the young men walked back to the barracks, discussing what had happened before they all turned in. It would be an early morning. The king was due to arrive soon.

Brian awoke early to the sound of the door opening. He cracked open one eye. The sky was just beginning to lighten. The air had a slight chill to it, reminding him of the colder weather to come in the not too distant future. He got up to stir the fire before the others got up, only to find Arden in the doorway with a dazed look on his face. He held a piece of paper in his hand.

THE BATTLE

"I found this nailed to the door," he explained as he handed the note to Brian. As Brian read the note, Arden quickly woke the others, holding his finger to silence them as Brian swore.

Brian ran for his pants and shirt, and carrying his shoes, he ran to his Sgian Dubh and dagger. Putting the Sgian Dubh in its sheath around his leg and the dagger at his waist, he ran out the door.

Arden explained to his friends as he turned to run to the keep, "It's a trap. They plan to kill Brian, and they have Ava. They will use Ava as exchange for Brian. I felt it on the note—the hatred and need for revenge. I must go to our fathers." He left at a run to relay what he had felt in the note. It stated Cearul wanted to meet Brian alone at the arena, a place in the middle of the forest with a large open space. It was often used by both clans to settle fights among the clan. When Arden touched the note, he received an image of many soldiers and Cearul holding Ava. Cearul had laid a trap using Ava. His man must have made it back and relayed what he saw. Brian was in love with Ava.

Pup and the rest of the young men gathered their weapons. Pup took charge as he stated, "We must have a plan; we cannot do this without help." Together, they came up with a plan and ran for the stables, taking the time to bridle the horses but not taking the time to saddle them.

BRIAN BROUGHT his big charger to a halt a mile before he arrived at the arena. He had learned, in his training, to be wary. He looked carefully at the land around him, seeing many cat tracks all around. Only another cat would see the blade of grass that was bent over or the claw marks on the trunks of trees. A single cat hair caught on a brush, a *black* hair. He could smell that many cats had passed here. This would be a fight to the death, and Cearul would call his faithful to his aid. Brian had no doubt that they would try and make it *his* death. He quickly turned to his cat form, feeling his bones change, his teeth elongate. Feeling the strength, he climbed the trees to get a better look. Carefully and quietly, he ran from tree to tree. As he approached the arena, he saw the many soldiers hiding in the forest all around, all armed with deadly weapons. Then he saw Cearul exit into the clearing, and what he saw made his blood run cold. Fear took his breath away as the evil leader led Ava into the middle of the clearing by the throat. Her feet were off the ground as he dragged her struggling to pull his arm away and allow her to breath. She twisted and turned but to no avail. She kicked and tried to bite, but nothing worked or gave her relief. Once they got to the middle of the clearing, he let her feet touch the ground, but he continued to hold her by the throat.

"Settle down, little human. We wait for Brian." He gave her an evil smile before he continued. "A human life is so fragile. It would be a shame to kill you before your lover gets to say goodbye."

Ava screamed when she finally could get some air. "My father will kill you for this. I am protected by the king. Don't you see my amulet? The king will skin you alive, very slowly, cat," she spat.

Cearul just laughed as he looked around in the trees. He spotted his victim as Brian jumped to the ground. Quickly changing back to human, he slowly walked to Cearul and said, "Let her go. It is me you want."

"No, little cat. I will kill her before your eyes as punishment for your disobedience all these years. Then, I will kill you slowly. Your line will die out, and I will rule both clans."

Brian continued walking to Cearul, but before he got too close, Cearul snapped his fingers and four guards came to take Brian. Brian fought hard, changing to cat. He knew Ava's life was at stake. He took out his Sgian Dubh from his boot and held it out, swiping at any of the guards who got close enough, but they circled him and came at him from all sides. Just when he thought it was useless, he heard his friends. They were just exiting the forest.

Pup held up his hand. "Stop! If it is a fight you want, make it fair." The four men ran to the guards who immediately turned to fight off the new threat.

Pup and the other three boys were making short work of the guards until Cearul roared out, "I will kill the girl."

The men all stopped, looking at a horrified Ava. She was again fighting to loosen Cearul's arm.

With a last kick to the guards, the men stepped back as Brian gave the order, "Stop and go home. This is my fight. Don't let them kill Ava." Tears formed in his eyes as he looked at the small girl in Cearul's grasp.

"Let her go, and I will go willingly. I will not fight you."

Cearul thought for a second before he smiled evilly again. "Agreed. Put down your weapons with your hands up and come to me. Ask me nicely to kill you and spare the girl."

Just then, galloping from the trees, came the lairds—all five of them, with Wolf in the lead. Rolland hopped off his horse and walked toward the clearing. Striding confidently and with purpose, he pointed his finger at Cearul and roared, "You dare to harm my daughter?"

Wolf gave the whistle for the wolves as he walked up to stand at

Rolland's side. The rest of the lairds followed. Wolf looked around at the soldiers in the forest before he called out, "Anyone who wants to swear loyalty to the king tomorrow, when he comes, will be welcome. You shall live. Leave now and go to Daniel. The rest will die. Let Ava go, Cearul, or you and your men will die a horrible death. That I promise you. Look around you."

As the men turned to look, they saw a hundred or more wolves. Their eyes were gleaming with death and their teeth sharp and dripping with drool. They heard Dylan lift his whistle and give the mournful sound that would bring the falcons that soon circled overhead. Dylan gave another whistle that brought the eagles, their sharp beaks and talons out and ready. Many of Cearul's men broke rank and ran for Daniel, swearing that they had families and needed them all to be protected. Daniel and Colin gathered them all and took them to their village to retrieve their families and then travel to the tabby keep.

Wolf again gave Cearul a last warning, "Let her go now; it is your last chance to save yourself."

Just as Cearul lifted his knife to Ava, a huge white-tailed eagle sailed down, taking Cearul's head in his huge talons. He picked him up, and as Cearul dropped Ava to grab for the talons sinking into his head, the eagle carried him up, his talons tearing ever deeper into the evil black cat's head. The screams of the cat as he tried to change but could not, because the eagle had him, were deafening. Squeezing his head, the talons dug deep into his skull until the eagle had carried him high above the trees and dropped him to the ground, dead. The guards who had stayed to witness this began to run, but the wolves, falcons and eagles made short work of them as they tried to escape their fate. Ava ran—not to Rolland but to Brian—crying. Her sobs wrenched his heart as he picked her up. Rolland stood scratching his head before a smile crawled across his face.

"Let us help Daniel get the rest of the black clan settled so we can relax the rest of the day. You know the king will keep us busy knighting and swearing in all these people, tomorrow. He should be here in the morn."

The lairds gathered their horses and galloped away, leaving the animals to take care of the bodies. The young men walked to their horses to the sounds of wailing and screams and the animals squawking and howling. Pup could tell by the look on Dylan's face that the carnage had taken a toll on the younger man. He put his arms around him and led him to his horse with these words of comfort, "You had no choice, Dylan. You had to save Ava. Da gave them all a chance to save themselves, but some men are just plain evil. Do not feel bad for using your gift for the good of all of us."

Dylan shook his head sadly. "I don't like being responsible for the killing of another man. I know it needed to be done; I just wish someone else could have done the deed."

Brian and Ava came to offer support to their friend, then.

"I thank you for saving my life, Dylan. That man was pure evil. I saw what he was capable of. He would have enjoyed killing Brian but, also, making all his and the tabby clan miserable. He would have made the tabbies suffer the same as his own people do now. I saw no soul in him."

Dylan looked at Ava in surprise. "No soul? How can that be?"

Ava shook her head. "He was evil," was all she could say. She had seen how bad the shifter really was, but she would not let anyone else know the demons she saw in him. She wanted Dylan to know that he did the world a favor.

Brian put his arm around his friend and added, "You save many lives today, my friend, and for that, I have to thank you."

Dylan shook his head in acceptance as he answered with, "No thanks needed, Brian. You know that."

The men mounted up and rode slowly back to the keep, Ava in front of Brian. His muscular arm was around her, giving her comfort and making her feel safe once again.

She explained to them as they rode that she had fallen asleep, only to be awakened by four men. They had bound and gagged her and lowered her to four more men below her bedroom window. Then, they had ridden, with her bound, to the black cat clan, where Cearul waited for her.

She leaned back into Brian's chest as tears formed in her eyes. "I knew they would ask for your life. I knew they would use me to kill you. I couldn't get away. You would have gladly given your life for me. I can feel it in you."

Brian held her even tighter and said, "I would protect you with my life. You are my mate. No matter that you are not a shifter. I feel it inside." He kissed the top of her head as they entered the huge gates around the bailey. The tabbies had set up many tents for their black cat guests by now. Tomorrow, they would swear allegiance to the king and Colin and then return home. Ava knew what would happen next, but she kept it to herself. Children and wives were found and brought in to their men to await the next day. All of them celebrated the end of Cearul's rule. Food was brought out to the large tables that were still set up. Drink was set out, along with milk for the children. There were blankets to keep them warm, as the nights were turning colder. Fires were built to help keep them warm, too. When all was as ready as possible, the lairds retired to the study to discuss the two weddings.

Amy ran to Pup and threw her arms around his neck, reaching up for a kiss before she informed Ava, "Seitka has four seamstresses to work on our wedding dresses. We must go and pick out the material and let them know exactly what we want. Our mothers are waiting for us. They are hoping our fathers finish the negotiations, so we can wed while the king is here. We must hurry. Come on." She dragged Ava with her to the keep and their waiting mothers.

Pup and Brian laughed at the girls, watching their cute little bottoms hurrying away. That is until Daniel grabbed both men by the arms and hurried them into the keep for the women to begin making their wedding clothes as well. The MacDonald plaid and the Tabby plaid were all laid out. The women were waiting to take the young men in the back room to measure them and then sew the material into a fine set of wedding clothes.

That night, as the sun was going down and the bailey was dotted with many campfires, the lairds finally came out of the study slapping one another on the back and laughing. The women had supper waiting for them in the great room.

Rolland put his arm around Brian. "We have the dowry worked out, but I had some questions. It seems no one knows what will happen when the two of you have children of your own. A shifter and a human have never fallen in love before, never married. I know my Ava loves you, and I respect you. It will work out. It's not the first time one of us has married someone with a special skill. The child may be a shifting seer, for all we know." He laughed at his own joke. "We will speak to the king when he arrives. Ava is the daughter of a laird, and as such, she needs the king's blessing, also."

Brian nodded with a smile that lit the room. "I understand, sir. I promise I will always protect her and love her and any children we may have."

Rolland replied, "She will be a handful. You do know that?" When Brian smiled, nodding his head, Rolland threw back his head and laughed. "You will know how to bring her around. I am sure I will be leaving her in capable hands. I'll leave you to discuss the necessities with your uncle. Good sleep and, hopefully, everything will be ready for the wedding in two days' time."

Brian went to his uncle, who was waiting for him in the study. Colin handed him a cup of whiskey.

THE MAN

"You are a man now, Brian. I want to tell you how proud I am of the way you have grown." He touched his cup to Brian's before they both took a sip. It burned as it went down the young man's throat and warmed his insides.

Colin gave Brian the amount of Ava's dowry. Brian choked as he took the next sip. Colin patted him on the back.

"Take it easy, lad, you bring a fair amount, too. Also, I am going to ask the king to make you the laird of the black cat clan. You are marrying an important laird's daughter, after all. Daniel will help you until you get your feet under you, but I have no doubt you will bring peace and prosperity to the black cat clan. We will live in harmony, finally. We will trade together and help one another, becoming allies, which will make us even stronger and more prosperous. It will also keep you close to home and to your mother. She has worried all these years that you would move to the abbey and she would rarely see you. She will now see her grandchildren grow."

Brian looked up from his drink to look his uncle in the eyes. "Thank you, sir. I will always try to make you and my family proud of me."

Colin patted him on the back. "There is much to do. Tomorrow, the king arrives early, according to the note I received from one of the carrier pigeons. We should seek our beds. We will see all of you at dawn."

Colin left with a proud smile on his face as Brian finished his drink in thoughtful contemplation.

A knock on the door roused him out of his thoughts. Pup entered with a smile on his face. "Let us seek our beds, brother."

The boys all walked to the barracks together chattering about the day's events. None of them noticed the chill in the air as they walked into the barracks and Brian started the fire. He lay in his bed, unable to sleep. His mind kept going over how brave his Ava was and how the day had turned out. He no longer feared Cearul. The monster was dead, after years of tormenting his people and him, his biological son. There would be peace, at last. Finally, late that night, he fell into a fitful sleep.

Everyone was awakened long before dawn when the commotion of many horses and tired men could be heard. The king had arrived, with his huge contingent of guards who accompanied him everywhere he went. The men laughing, discussing arrangements, and quieting a skittish horse were all evidence of his arrival. The young men quickly dressed to be of assistance, finding the guards places to sleep. There were two long barracks with a kitchen and many beds lined against the wall, with a well-stocked fireplace in each. Dylan and Sean went to each, lighting the fires to warm the barracks for the men who would soon occupy them.

Pup and Brian went to awaken the cooks for each barracks. They set to work to quickly make tea and breakfast for the guards who were lucky enough to be able to sleep for a few hours afterwards. Some would yet pull guard duty. They would switch after a few hours, so all of them had a few hours of sleep, at least. The king's page and servants would stay in the room next to his in the keep. His sleeping quarters were made ready earlier. After a couple hours, everything was again quiet, and everyone got a couple more hours of sleep before dawn.

Brian got up before the rest and dressed quickly in the morning chill. He stirred the fire and left for the keep to help his uncle and his mother. When he arrived, the cooks were setting the table for the campers outside, with huge platters of ham and eggs and hot oats and milk and tea. The campers were just rising and seeing to their children. Inside, the cooks were making a different breakfast —one fit for a king. Ham, bacon, fluffy scrambled eggs and sweet cakes to eat and coffee, tea and juice to drink. Brian looked up to see Amanda walking down the stairs arm in arm with no other than the king, himself. He was in awe, frozen to the spot at the sight of them.

When Amanda sat next to her royal uncle and poured him a steaming cup of coffee, she looked at Brian with a smile. "Good morning, Brian. Have you met my godfather, the king?"

Brian stammered for an answer, tongue tied and looking for his voice, when Wolf came in and slapped him on the back.

"Come, sit, Brian. The king and you and I have some things to talk about."

Brian sat across from the king of England and Wolf and discussed becoming the laird of the black cat clan. The king listened to Wolf carefully and with respect as Wolf told him what had happened the day before.

"Do you think you are ready to become a laird, Brian?" he asked the young man.

Daniel had come to sit next to Brian as Brian answered honestly, "I will need the help of my father, until I can get my bearings. But I think I am ready to be a good laird, a much better one than the one they had."

Rolland and the rest had arrived soon after the discussion began, and everyone had a hearty breakfast. All the lairds explained to the king how Brian had trained with them and had become a man to be proud of.

The king sat back in his chair with his hand over his aging and large stomach. Finally, he said, "I think it is a good idea to have Brian become the laird. He is, after all, half black cat. It will stabilize this region. I will need to knight you, Brian, and the rest of you young men. I also hear there are to be two weddings. One of which is my own great-nephew's."

He paused, took a drink of tea, and continued. "I also want the allegiance of all the black cats, as well as every one of the tabby clan. In return, I will give each clan purebred beef cattle and milk cows to breed and to feed you all. I will have the feed and men to help build the barns necessary sent to you as soon as Maria can send a message back to the castle. I will leave some of my guards to begin the building. They will help you, but everyone is going to need to work together to get the barns done and filled before winter. It is already heading to autumn. I would have my men at home ready the cattle and start for here as soon as possible. It is quite a distance. The cattle move slowly, so as not to lose too much weight before they arrive. I think, in the spring, I will send some men to help build a healing building and a hospital. You will need to find a healer and send them to Seitka to train. If we build one between the two clans, it will help to bring them together, also. The sooner Seitka can train them, the better."

Seitka beamed at the confidence the king had in her, while Brian looked at his mother with pride. She had endured hard times because of Cearul and she had come through it stronger than ever.

The king continued with his thoughts. "I would like for Brian and the rest of you to join me at the abbey next spring, to discuss further what may be needed. I want to keep in touch via Wolf and the other lairds. If possible, I would like a few of you to spend some of the summer at the abbey. Take turns, if you wish, but we need to all be connected. We need to work together and face problems together. That is the reason I am so happy that Brian will marry Ava. It will keep the connection strong. Is there anything I have forgotten? The girls have their amulets already, of course. The wedding will be tomorrow, and the swearing will be after. The knighting of Brian and the rest of the men will be after the swearing. Now, I would like to rest my weary bones for a few hours more, if you don't mind. I am getting too old for all this traveling." He turned to Wolf and Amanda. "I will expect you again in the spring, as usual? Your aunt sends her best and begs me to convey how much she misses you and the children."

Amanda patted his hand as she confirmed they would see them in the spring as they did every year. The elderly royal got up and wearily walked up the steps to his room again.

Amanda looked worriedly at Wolf before she whispered, "He is getting older. I hate to say it, but soon, he will not be able to travel. Jeremy will have to take over more of his duties."

Wolf looked his wife in the eye with compassion. He knew Amanda loved this man, but he was aging, it was true. "We will visit him and your aunt more often if you wish, wife. Pup has shown he is man enough to watch over the clan while we are gone for a month, here and there. Aaron can help out, too. Jeremy is a good man; he will be a good leader and king someday. Hopefully, not *too* soon."

Amanda gave her husband's hand a squeeze in thanks.

The day was a busy one with the seamstresses finishing the wedding clothes and food to prepare for so many. A stage had been erected so everyone could see the weddings, the alliances and the knighting. It went quickly, and before they knew it, the day was gone, and everyone turned in early.

The next day started even earlier. Breakfast was a quick meal, but dinner promised to be a huge affair. Daniel and Wolf had hefted two large boars over large spits and began roasting them over the fires. Rolland, Acelin and Jamie hefted two calves over two other spits with a fire under them as well. Potatoes were put into the coals to cook as were ears of corn. The cooks had worked late into the night on cakes and puddings, along with many loaves of fresh bread. Kegs of mead and whiskey were made ready to fill many cups, with pitchers of milk on the tables for the children. The fiddler and bagpipe players were tuning up, and Colin had found some jugglers for the children. The morning was clear but had a bite in the air. The early mist still hung heavy over the bailey, reminding all that autumn was on the way. The festivities started right after breakfast. All the lairds and their families sat on the stage with the king. The two young men waited for their brides on the stage, along with the priest who had been brought in to officiate.

Brian looked nervously around, waiting for his bride, and when he saw Amy leaving the keep first to stand next to Pup, he knew Ava was next. When she walked out the door, the sight took his breath away. She was beautiful. Her dress was blue to match her violet eyes. Her hair was styled in ringlets with flowers woven through the curls. He only had eyes for her as she walked up the steps to stand next to him.

The ceremony began, and it wasn't long before it was over. Brian felt like the luckiest man in the world as the king announced them married.

His Majesty then turned to the crowd. "It is my intention to make Brian the laird over the black cat clan. Is there any good objection?"

The cheering could be heard for miles. The noise of happiness scared the birds out of the trees, and Brian's heart swelled. These would be his people. He would see them prosper and come to love him and his family. He would finally belong and feel welcomed.

Brian knelt on one knee as the king knighted him Sir Brian of the Tabby and the Black clans. Pup was next to be knighted, and the rest of their friends walked up the stairs, one at a time, to become knights of the realm, also.

When the boys had all been knighted, the king turned to the crowd and said, "I want you all to pledge your allegiance to me, the King of England. In return, I will give you not only my protection but cattle and milk cows, so all may have meat and milk. I will also help build your barns and fill them with enough feed for the winter. In the spring, I will build you an abbey with a hospital like the one we have near the four corners. The hospital and abbey will be built between the two clans, so both can use them. Before we leave, my guards will help you build your smokehouses and barns. I will help you get ready for winter. No one will be hungry or cold. My soldiers will help you gather wood. If any do not want to pledge to me, you will be allowed to take your families and leave. Make no mistake, pledge or no, I will not tolerate anyone tearing down what we will build here. I will protect what is ours."

The crowd cheered, and he went on to say, "Anyone who wants to pledge to the crown may come up. Tell me your name, so it may be recorded. Form a line at the bottom of the steps and let us begin."

It took until dinnertime to finish all the pledges. Every one of the black cats was happy to align with the king.

Daniel stood up before everyone was allowed to go to the tables to feast and announced, "If anyone needs help with thatching their roofs, patching their homes, or fixing any buildings they need to get through the winter, come now and let us know, so we may help you. If you need vegetables or milk until the cows arrive, stop and let us know. We mean it when we say we will help you get through the winter. Come spring, we will help you prosper. We will help you get your fields ready or start a business. We have a need for inns and shoemakers, and there are many other business opportunities we can explore. Think of what you would like to do to earn your keep during the winter, and we will talk about it in the spring. Brian and Ava will stay here until we can fix the laird's keep and make it habitable for the new laird."

Everyone cheered again before heading toward the food. For the first time in a very long time, the black cats had hope for a better future.

That night, the music played, the ale flowed, and the food was plenty to celebrate the weddings of the king's great nephew and the new laird. Many of the black cat clan stopped to introduce themselves to Brian and ask him and Daniel and Colin many questions. The men answered them the best they could and promised help to those who needed it. Some asked for help for some for the elderly who had stayed back because they were too old to travel. Brian promised to visit the next day and see what needed to be done. One young man about his age volunteered to give them a tour and introduce them to the elderly and handicapped. Edward would be up early to take them around and introduce everyone to the ones who had to stay behind. Brian made a note to keep an eye on Edward as he may make a good second. He seemed caring of his people and honest. Everyone enjoyed the night before making sure the fires were hot enough to keep them warm through the night.

Brian and Pup looked at each other early in the evening. They would turn in early, finding it hard to control themselves as they waited for their wedding nights to start.

Not long after the dancing began, Pup and Brian took their brides by the hand and led them to the buggy waiting for them—complete with shoes tied to the back. They would ride the short distance to Daniel and Seitka's home for their first night. Seitka had lovingly prepared the two bedrooms with flowers for the girls and plenty of wood and food. Seitka and Daniel would stay at the keep for the night.

As soon as the couples arrived, the maids and cooks readied to leave, telling the men if they needed anything, they would be in the maids' quarters in the cabin next door. Snacks of cold meat and cheeses and pastries were set out on the table. The fireplace glowed with fire and warmth. Each bedroom had its own fireplace that was also burning, making both bedrooms nice and warm. A hot bath was waiting in each, along with an expensive bottle of wine and two glasses. Fluffy towels and washcloths were warmed and ready. The men carried their wives up the stairs to their own bedrooms and closed the doors.

~

BRIAN PUT AVA DOWN, letting her toes touch the floor before he bent down to taste her lips. She blushed so prettily, it brought a smile to his lips. He slowly turned her and untied her clothes, letting her beautiful wedding dress pool at her feet before he picked it up and carefully laid it on the bureau. He took her pins out of her hair, one at a time, slowly. It fell like a silken curtain down to her bottom. After she had stepped out of all her clothes, he led her to the bath. He quickly shed his own clothes, folding them neatly and putting them with her wedding dress. He slowly turned to her, giving her the first look at her husband's nakedness. Her eyes traveled slowly down to his manhood, where they opened in shock. "Husband, that will not fit in me," she said.

"How do you know where it is to fit, young lady?"

Her face flamed with shame as she looked down to the floor. "I followed you and Pup when you went with the MacFinnely twins."

Now, it was Brian's turn to open his eyes in shock. "You followed us to the barn and watched as Pup and I, um, made love to Trixie and Micky?"

A small smile showed on her beautiful lips, which she quickly covered. She looked up into his eyes. "Amy and I both followed you. We watched what you did. Please don't tell our das," she begged.

Brian shook his head in wonder. "You get into the bath. I must tell Pup. Both of you girls have earned a spanking. I will return in just a few seconds."

As he quickly put on his robe and left the room, Ava looked worriedly at the door before she quickly got into the hot tub. The water was delightful. She found a bar of lavender soap next to the tub and lathered her skin, enjoying the luxury of a hot bath. She had just rinsed the soap from her hair when Brian came back in. Shedding his robe, he slowly climbed in behind her. Taking the soap and cloth, he began to wash her back, starting at her neck and working his way down to her bottom.

"Turn around and face me, my love."

She turned, and he began to lather his hands, running them over her collar to her breasts, where he took his time, twisting her nipples with his sudsy hands until she began to squirm. His sudsy hands moved lower to her stomach and down further until they came to her pussy. He made sure to rub her little love button before he stuck one finger inside her. He then took the washcloth and rinsed her as she began to squirm even more.

"Stand, so I can rinse you thoroughly."

She stood as he rinsed her, including her pussy, making sure to rub her bundle of nerves with the rough cloth.

"Spread your legs further, so I can do a good job," he instructed. She obeyed, tilting her head back as the tingly feeling began to warm her insides.

"Now, you may sit and wash me."

She started with his neck, the same as he had done, but did not stop at his breasts like he did to hers. She went right down to his cock that was standing straight out of the water. She gently washed it and went lower to his testicles. She put the cloth back into the water and soaped her hands to massage them gently before picking up the cloth and rinsing him. Her hand wrapped around his manhood, her fingers not able to touch as she circled it.

"Very good. Now, I will get out and retrieve the towel I have warming over the chair by the fire."

He got up and retrieved his towel first, drying himself before he came for her with the other. He then dried her carefully, rubbing her scalp when he got to her beautiful hair. He led her to the chair in front of the fire, sitting her down before he retrieved the brush. He began to brush her hair gently, careful not to pull it or get it caught in a snarl. When it finally dried, silky soft to the touch, he put the brush away. Helping her to her feet, he led her to the bed where he laid her down on top of the blankets. He crawled in behind her.

Sitting up on his elbow, he looked at her and said, "You have been very naughty, spying on us, little one. I have to spank you for it. Roll over on your tummy, so I can begin your punishment."

Ava looked warily at him before she slowly rolled over, presenting her bottom for her spanking. She looked over her shoulder sadly and pleaded, "Please don't spank me too hard, Brian. It was a long time ago, and I didn't need to tell you. I didn't want to start our marriage with a secret."

"I realize that, little one. Do you trust me to give you just what you need and no more? I will be the man of the house, and you will obey me or suffer the consequences. You do understand, don't you?"

With a sigh, Ava nodded her head. She knew how her parents and all the other parents lived their lives. The men had the final word. Their word was law, and if their wives misbehaved, they were spanked.

Brian took his time. He began by rubbing her bottom and explaining to her that he would not put up with her mischievousness any longer. He would not put up with her putting herself in danger or lying to him, in any shape or form. When he was sure that she understood, he began.

The sting of the first spank surprised her. She tried to put her hand back to protect her bottom, but Brian caught it easily enough, holding it with one hand. The other was trapped between them. He began in earnest. Not too hard, just enough to sting and begin to warm her bottom, causing a heat to build down below. Spank, sting, gentle rub. Repeat. It continued until her bottom began to burn. Her womanhood began to weep its love juices. Brian began to build his fire. Inside and out, she began to burn, until, finally, when she felt like her bottom would burst into flame and she couldn't help but let out a sob, he stopped. Turning her over, he placed her on her stinging, hot bottom as he reached for and inserted first one finger and then two.

"Tsk, tsk, young lady, you are sopping wet for me. I will have to do something to help you."

He positioned himself between her legs and began plucking her nipples, bending down to suck the other as he worked on one and then its twin.

Ava twisted and turned, moaning for relief as his tongue made a trail lower over her flat stomach down to her hungry pussy. He lapped at her button, making her squeal.

Finally, Ava began to beg, "Please, Brian, do something. Something in me wants to come out, but I don't know what. Help me, Brian, I want to...I need to do something. I can't stand it. Do something."

Brian positioned his cock at her entrance, stopping to explain to her, "This will hurt, the first time. I cannot stop it. I will promise I will only bring you pleasure ever after."

She thrashed back and forth, not caring.

He sank his massive cock inside her to the hilt.

Ava felt a sting inside, but as Brian began to move faster, the sting was quickly replaced by a burning need and a feeling of fullness.

Brian began to pound into her, telling her, "I cannot be gentle this first time, my sweet Ava. Forgive me, I promise better next time."

Ava felt something monumental coming from inside. She felt a tightness. She lifted her hips to meet his as he continued until, suddenly, she felt the world tilt. She felt herself explode from within. Just as she gave out a great squeal, calling Brian's name and grabbing his shoulders, she came apart. She heard Brian give out a mighty roar as he continued to pump into her. When they had both finished, their breaths coming in great gulps, he quickly moved off of her and went to get the cloth to wash them both before returning to bed. He pulled her into his arms, her head over his heart. After covering them both with the blanket, they fell into a deep satisfied sleep.

Brian woke her twice more that night. Each time they made

love, it was sweeter than the last. They talked in between, of things like children and where she wanted to live.

"I will take you to the black cats' keep. If you don't think it can be changed to suit you, we can build another. We'll take the other men with us to see if the great wall needs to be fixed to keep us, our children, and the clan safe. If any of the other clansman or women need help fixing their huts for the winter, we will help them. I will keep an eye on Edward. I have a feeling he could become a good second, and I will need an ally in the clan for a bit, until we prove we have the best intentions for them."

"I will touch him when he is unaware and see if I can feel or see some of how he really feels," she offered.

"Thank you, my darling. I would like to ask you to keep your gift a secret for a while. We could use it to our advantage."

Ava agreed, and they both fell asleep once again, only waking to the pounding of the door.

It was Pup. "Come on, you two, the day is half done. We have much to do."

Ava groaned, "I will kill that man."

Brian chuckled, giving her a sharp slap on the bottom. " The sun is high in the sky. We are slug-a-beds." He got up and found he had clothes, as did Ava, in the wardrobe. Quickly dressing, he pulled the blankets off his wife. Giving her a kiss on the cheek, he left her with a smile. Pup had gotten the cooks to make an early meal for them before they left for the keep.

The girls chattered the whole way home, while Brian explained to Pup what he wanted to do that day. He asked Pup and the other men for their help.

Brian noticed that Dylan was gone, and so was Caitlan. He scratched his head as he mentioned it to the rest of the men.

Danny told him, "Dylan is struggling with the killing. I saw him and Caitlan walking to the pond." He nodded to the sky. The falcons were circling over where he was sure Dylan and Caitlan were.

Pup looked at the rest of the men and asked, "Sean, does Chance know about Dylan struggling with this?"

Sean nodded. "I told him, this morning. He looked concerned and he said he would talk to Maria, since she has had this gift since birth. I hope they can figure something out."

"I am going to stroll quietly down to the pond and see if I can tell what is going on," Pup stated.

Brian shook his head. "This is my home. I know how to see what is going on without either of them knowing. I'll change to cat and go through the trees. I will return shortly."

All agreed, leaving Brian to take Ava with him to the tree line.

"I will show you what it looks like when I change. I'll return to you very shortly."

Ava agreed and watched in wonder as her husband began the change. His bones shifted, and he quickly grew the most beautiful striped fur. She ran her hands through it and marveled at the softness.

Brian rubbed against her leg, putting his scent on her and marking her, so all the other cats knew she was taken before he bounded into the trees. Hopping from branch to branch, careful not to make a sound or disturb a leaf, he carefully made his way to the pond. When he arrived, his heart swelled. On the hill over-looking the pond sat Caitlan with Dylan. Dylan had his head on her lap as she played with his hair. He could hear Caitlin's voice travel over the air, soft and comforting as she stopped to listen to Dylan and his concerns. It was such a touching scene that Brian felt like an intruder. He carefully backed away and returned the way he came, down to his waiting Ava. He dressed and walked back to their friends and he explained what he had seen.

Pup, at first, was upset and ready to go to his sister, but Amy stopped him. "They need each other now. Let them be, and perhaps soon, there will be another wedding in our group. I think that would be wonderful."

Ava agreed, "He needs this now. He saved my life, but I think it took a piece of his own soul. Let Caitlan help him, and his parents, of course. I think this will not be the first time he will be called on to use his skill."

The dark, loud voice of Wolf scared the girls who did not see him quietly walking up to them.

"There will not be two weddings so soon. Caitlan is too young. Pup, go to your sister. Give her some time but not too long. You understand? Give her the time to help Dylan. I owe him my son's life, also, but not too much time. If she hasn't returned in an hour, go to her."

Pup nodded his head.

Chance came up behind Wolf. "We will talk to him tonight, too. I think you're right. This will not be the last time he is asked to use his skill."

Colleen and Rolland came behind Danny before they looked at Ava and said, "Let us go to the other keep. Your mother would help you decide whether it can be made to suit you. We will all go to see what needs to be done in the village to make everyone warm and safe for the winter. The king is talking to Colin while some of his guards go with us."

Acelin and Hope agreed as they walked toward Amy. Hope put her arm around her daughter. "It will give us girls time to talk." She bent down to whisper to Ava and Amy, "Colleen and I would like to have some time alone with you, in case you have any questions that are unanswered."

The girls agreed, and the men went to retrieve the wagons loaded with tools and their horses. The guards followed with more tools and lumber. Just as they were about to leave and Pup was about to go find his sister, Caitlan and Dylan came walking arm in arm through the gate to the bailey.

They all jumped into one of the wagons, and off they went to the black cat clan.

Wolf shook his head in wonder at how he and Amanda had lost

two children to their mates in one month's time. He looked towards home. He was ready to return.

The king had agreed to leave and see to the shipping of the cattle and lumber. There was not much else to do. "I am too old to stray too far from home anymore, my children." He smiled as he looked at all the sons and daughters. Look how wonderfully my experiment all those years ago worked out. I am so pleased."

Amanda laughed and gave her godfather a hug. "It did, didn't it? You are such a wise man. Tell Aunt Charlotte we will come for a visit in the spring. I think my husband would be happy to stay home most of the time now, too. We have to build Pup and Amy a new home before winter. Wolf said Pup is old enough to take over as laird when we are gone for a while. Aaron will help him, and so will the other lairds. We are a team to be reckoned with. Soon, we will all be intertwined. I am pleased, too."

Wolf came up and took a sip of his wife's lips, giving her a pat on the bottom. "Are you ready, wife? We have much to do so that we may go home soon." He gave the king a wink and a wave as he guided his wife out the door.

The king turned to Colin with a smile on his face. Everything was working out wonderfully, and he took all the credit.

THE END

CHAR CAULEY

I am a happily married mother of three sons and two kitties. I live in a very small town (unincorporated) in Wisconsin. I love to garden, write and of course read. I also work in a glass factory with robots. Writing is a lifelong dream come true.

Don't miss these exciting titles by Char Cauley and Blushing Books!

Healer Series
Amanda's Wolf – Book 1
Colleen's Laird – Book 2
Little Hope's Doctor – Book 3
Seitka's Shifter - Book 4

Daughters of Samual Fox Series
Spring's Savior - Book 1
Summer's Lawman - Book 2
Autumn's Doctor - Book 3
Wynter's Storm - Book 4
Willow's Journey - Book 5

Audiobooks
Amanda's Wolf

Milton Keynes UK
Ingram Content Group UK Ltd.
UKHW011850150124
436080UK00001B/22